"A SHIP!" CRIED THE SAILOR ON LOOKOUT DUTY.

"Where away?" the captain called back.

"Fine on the larboard bow," the lookout answered.

I could see nothing from the deck. Captain Hunter scrambled up the shrouds, though, and stared off to the east. "It's the *Fury*," he called down at last, and I breathed a little easier. The *Fury* was a sloop under the command of John Barrel, a right, true buccaneer and a friend of ours from back in the early part of the year.

Captain Hunter slid down a backstay like a boy, dropped to the deck, and ordered, "Clear for action."

And then, with surprising speed, the *Fury* shifted her sails, spun about to show us her broadside, and opened fire!

Read all the Pirate Hunter stories.

Book One: *Mutiny!*
Book Two: *The Guns of Tortuga*
Book Three: *Heart of Steele*

PIRATE HUNTER

Heart of
Steele

Brad Strickland and Thomas E. Fuller

ALADDIN PAPERBACKS

New York London Toronto Sydney Singapore

This book is lovingly dedicated to my youngest son, John Douglas
Fuller.
—*Thomas E. Fuller*

And to Thomas's daughter Christina, his "pickle princess."
—*Brad Strickland*

First Aladdin Paperbacks edition July 2003

Text copyright © 2003 by Brad Strickland and Thomas E. Fuller

Illustrations copyright © 2003 by Dominic Saponaro

ALADDIN PAPERBACKS
An imprint of Simon & Schuster
Children's Publishing Division
1230 Avenue of the Americas
New York, NY 10020

Designed by Debra Sfetsios
The text of this book was set in Minion.

Printed in the United States of America
2 4 6 8 10 9 7 5 3 1

Library of Congress Control Number 2002113758
ISBN 0-689-85298-3

PIRATE HUNTER

Heart of Steele

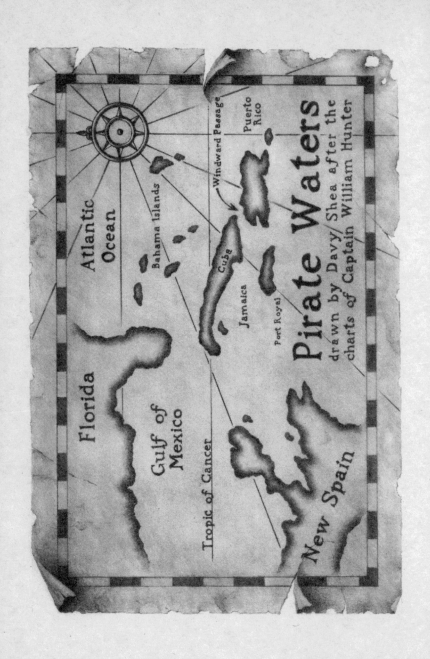

Pirate Waters

drawn by Davy/Shea after the
charts of Captain William Hunter

Atlantic
Ocean

Bahama Islands

Florida

Gulf of
Mexico

Tropic of Cancer

New Spain

Cuba

Jamaica

Port Royal

Windward Passage

Puerto
Rico

Main Mast

Mizzen

Fore

Rigging

Crows Nest

Captain's Cabin

Stern

Bow

In Deadly Waters

My name is Davy Shea. When my mother died in March 1687, leaving me an orphan, I left England and went to live with my uncle Patrick Shea of Port Royal, Jamaica. Uncle Patrick was a respected surgeon. Though he had a fine, high Irish temper, he was kind to me and began to educate me so that when I grew up, I might become a medical man.

But that plan seemed ruined when he and William Hunter mutinied and turned pirate, setting out on the French-built frigate *Aurora* to savage the ships in the West Indies. At least, I thought that was what was happening. Then I learned that it was all a plan by the former buccaneer Sir Henry Morgan to bring to justice the notorious pirate Jack Steele. We were not true pirates, but were secret agents of King James II. We were pirate hunters.

We sailed for months, until the day we engaged the great Spanish warship *Concepcíon*. With our ship battered, we made our way to the island of

Tortuga in the company of John Barrel, a brave and swaggering pirate who trusted us. In Tortuga, we learned that two English officers were being held for ransom, and Captain Hunter was determined to rescue them. One prisoner, alas, was murdered by Jack Steele. The other, to our surprise, turned out to be no man at all, but a Miss Helena Fairfax in disguise—and her "servant boy" turned out to be Jessie Cochran, the daughter of our landlady back in Port Royal, a girl who always found ways of tormenting me and my heart.

But we also learned that Jack Steele was gathering a pirate armada in Tortuga Harbor. We made a desperate alliance with the Spanish captain of the *Concepción*. In a pitched battle, Captain Hunter broke up the pirate fleet, but now Steele knew that we would never fight on his side. From that moment on, he knew he had a deadly enemy in William Hunter.

And we were about to find out just how deadly Steele could be on the day our lookout spied a floating wreck of a ship in the distance. . . .

CHAPTER 1

The Derelict

"A SHIP!"

The cry came drifting down from the maintop, almost like a leaf falling from a canvas tree. I lifted my head from the coil of rope where I lay dozing. The air felt hot and heavy, as it had for more than a week. What breeze there was barely served to move the frigate *Aurora* forward. It was the summer of 1688 and the Caribbees simmered like a buccaneer's barbeque.

"On deck, there! A ship!"

The cry came again and I squinted up the tall stepped lines of the mainmast to where wiry old Abel Tate stood watch in the maintop. Around me I could hear other members of the *Aurora*'s crew bestirring themselves, struggling up from where they had lain languid in the heat. It was all I could do to haul myself to my feet, but the idea of anything that might offer escape from the usual dreaded doldrums finally got me out of my comfortable coil. I staggered over to where my friend Mr. Jeffers, the gunner, stood, shading his single good eye from the sun with one callused hand.

"Devil can I see a thing," he muttered. "It could be whale, rock, or ship for I might swear!" Even with the sweat pouring into my own eyes, I had to smile. If he were aiming his beloved cannons, Mr. Jeffers had the eyes of a sea eagle. Otherwise he was as blind as a bat in a well.

I heard the stamp of boots on the quarterdeck above us and two voices—one light and laughing, the other rumbling and complaining. The laughing voice belonged to our captain, Mad William Hunter, the noted pirate hunter. The grumbling one was that of my uncle, Patrick Shea, the noted surgeon and pessimist. Once they clapped eyes on me, the two would think of one thousand and one errands and chores to keep me from anything dangerous—

or interesting. I grasped an idea and felt energy start to flow back into my sweat-drenched body. Uncle Patch says idle hands are the devil's workshop. That may be, but it takes a bit of inspiration to actually use the tools.

"Perhaps it just takes a younger eye, Mr. Jeffers," I said in my most innocent voice, which never seems to fool anyone for some reason. Mr. Jeffers turned and raised one ragged eyebrow in my direction. "And, of course, a bit of height." I let my own eyes drift upward. Mr. Jeffers's gaze followed my gaze and a broad grin spread across his scarred face.

"Aye, Davy, lad! Up ye go and send us back true word! That fool Tate would be sighting London Bridge if he thought he could!"

Quick as thought, I was out of my shoes and scurrying up the mainmast shrouds, my toes clutching the ratlines as I climbed. I heard a distant bellow that could have been Uncle Patch—or a bear amazed to find itself at sea. As long as I didn't look down, I could honestly say I couldn't tell which. So I climbed on and the gun deck of the *Aurora* fell away beneath me.

The higher I rose, the stronger the breezes driving

our ship forward became. After the humid listlessness of the past weeks, it felt like a swim in a cold river. I found myself climbing faster and faster until at last I reached Mr. Tate in his lofty perch atop the great central mainmast.

"What's the news, Mr. Tate?" I gasped out, drawing the cool air into my laboring lungs. "Mr. Jeffers has sent me up to find out what's what."

"Figured it wasn't the cap'n," he grumbled back. "Cap'n Hunter's got two good eyes in his head. Bartholomew Jeffers couldn't see the end of his own nose with a spyglass!" He turned and grinned at me. "'Course, a good glass might help someone else to use the good sight God gave them."

With that, he slapped his own glass into my hands and pointed carefully off to starboard. "There lies a bark, Davy, where the sea meets sky, or I'm a Barbary ape, I am!"

Quickly I extended the glass and scanned the horizon where his finger pointed, straight off the starboard bow. It took a second or two for my eye to adjust and a few after that to find her, but there she was, on the far horizon and low in the water. Too low.

"No wonder Mr. Jeffers couldn't see her," I cried. "All her masts are down!"

"Aye, 'twas only pure luck that I spied her in the first place! Not a stump above her railings. Could have been a reef for all she showed!"

"Could she have wrecked in a storm, Mr. Tate?"

"If storm it was, she had it all to herself, she did! Not a hint of wind did we have until this morning! You tell the cap'n it weren't no storm that stripped her. He has the word of Abel Tate on that!"

I started to fly back down the lines, as fast as I could move hands and feet. If no storm had dismasted that lonely hulk on the horizon, then only one other thing could have.

Pirates.

"Steady about, Mr. Warburton," Captain Hunter said to our hulking helmsman. Mr. Warburton was almost seven feet tall in any direction you cared to go. Right now, that formidable man was licking his lips and looking decidedly nervous.

"Don't like the look o' her, Cap'n. Don't like the look o' her at all."

"True, she's not at her best, but we shouldn't hold

that against her." Since there were no other ships about—and because the heat was so beastly—Captain Hunter had left his gaudy pirate costume hanging in his cabin. Instead of his wonderful emerald green jacket and yellow silk sash, he stood there in white trousers and billowing shirt. He looked annoyingly fresh and alert. I could smell myself all too well.

"Not what I meant," muttered Mr. Warburton. "Not what I meant at all." He chewed on his lower lip as if it was some kind of sugar treat. Mr. Warburton could snap a longboat oar across his leg like a huge matchstick. When cannonballs and shot had been whizzing around his head at the battle in Tortuga Harbor, he hadn't budged an inch. But the huge helmsman had one flaw: He was terrified of ghosts.

And if anything ever looked haunted, it was the wallowing hulk we sailed toward.

"Steady on, Mr. Warburton," grumped my uncle Patch from the other side of the captain. "I've never known a ghost to venture forth in the broad daylight. Not even Irish ones."

"There you have it," said Captain Hunter with a

laugh. "If even contrary Irish ghosts won't dance in daylight, then in daylight are we safe!"

"Less'n she was done in by a sea serpent," muttered Mr. Warburton under his breath. "Right fond o' rippin' out masts, yer sea serpent."

"If it was a sea serpent, then it used the masts for toothpicks, and I find that even harder to believe in than ghosts," the captain said, staring through his own spyglass. "Even Irish ones."

"You've just never been properly introduced to one, William," said my uncle, a rather nasty smile on his face. "Now there be ghosts in parts of County Clare . . ."

From my mother I had heard all about the Wan Pale Lady of County Clare. Since my uncle now began to talk of that well-known ghost, I went to stand at the railing and watch as we approached the derelict. The going was slow, there being barely enough breeze to move us at all. It took close to two hours to get within hailing range of her. And the closer we got, the quieter the crew became until I heard no sound at all except the waves and the creaking of the *Aurora*'s masts and lines. Something was horribly wrong with the derelict. The wrongness radiated out from her like ripples from a rock tossed into a pond. I breathed a sigh of relief when at last I saw movement on the decks, thinking that at least there were living people there.

Mr. Adams, the first mate, was preparing to hail her when Captain Hunter placed a hand on his arm. "Hold a minute, if you please, Mr. Adams." He gestured over to Giles Conway, an ex-marine and the best shot with a musket we had on board. "Are you loaded and primed, Mr. Conway?"

"Aye, Cap'n, never knows when somethin' untoward might come about, sir."

"An excellent philosophy, Mr. Conway. Would you oblige me with a shot over the decks of our crippled friend?"

Mr. Conway shrugged, sighted his long musket, then frowned and looked back at the captain. "Should I be aiming at anything in particular, sir? Seems right strange, otherwise, if ye get my drift?"

"Just fire, Mr. Conway. A nice loud bang is what we chiefly require."

Mr. Conway shrugged again, sighted carefully over the sides and gently squeezed off a shot. The sharp, loud crack echoed out across the water, and as soon as it did, the decks of the derelict vanished in a swirling, billowing cloud of white. Hundreds of gulls went screaming up into the air, their harsh cries ripping through the hot, still air. Up and up they spiraled, complaining all the way, not so much like a cloud as like smoke billowing up from a fire.

Then the wind shifted ever so slightly and a horrible smell came drifting over to us. I nearly gagged, and watched as hardened pirates covered their faces with their scarves and hands. Once as a boy in Bristol I had run an errand for my mother that had taken me close to a slaughterhouse. It was the same smell, only much worse. Everyone stared at the gently rocking derelict as the gulls screamed away. Then we drew close enough to make out her name written large across her stern.

The *Elizabeth Bingham*.

Finally Captain Hunter's voice broke through the terrible silence. "Best get your things together, Patch, in case someone over there has need of your services."

"I wish I felt there might be such aboard her," my uncle replied, crossing himself as he did. "But

I fear they'll be more in need of stout canvas bags and a round of shot to send them properly home. If anything but gulls lives yonder, then I am no human creature."

With the solemnity of a funeral the crew lowered a couple of boats over the side and prepared to close the distance between the two ships. Captain Hunter solemnly turned command of the *Aurora* over to Mr. Adams and swung himself lightly down into the first boat. Uncle Patch was supervising the lowering of his medical chest into the other and gingerly preparing to follow it. Uncle Patch never could get the knack of getting on or off a ship. Just as he was about to disappear over the side, he locked eyes on me and his rough face got the strangest look on it.

"Well, don't just hang about. 'Tis help I'll be needing if any be alive!" His emerald-green eyes closed for a moment and then flew open. "And if none be, then it's a lesson you'll not find in any book, David Michael Shea!"

I scrambled after him, eager to learn what lesson the *Elizabeth Bingham* had to teach me.

I wished I had stayed on the *Aurora*.

Across we went, the air still and dead, the slight breeze that had moved the *Aurora* faded. Slowly the starboard side of the *Elizabeth Bingham* began to loom above us, but not as high as it should have. She bobbed low in the water, draped in the remains of her masts and sails, all caught in a tangle of broken lines and shrouds. The foul smell grew stronger the closer we got to the crippled bark. A few gulls, braver than the rest, still patrolled the railings, eyeing us with an arrogance that made me shudder. Then we bumped up against her side and there was nothing for us to do but to clamber up the trailing ropes.

"Oh, blessed Mary and all the saints in heaven," breathed Uncle Patch as we dropped onto the deck and stood huddled together like children. I could say nothing at all. I felt as though I might never say anything ever again. I had spent months sailing with my uncle as his loblolly boy, helping him treat and sew up injured and dying men. Aye, and I had seen death, helped sew it into shrouds. That was nothing like the sight before us.

The crew and passengers of the *Elizabeth Bingham* lay tumbled on the deck of their crippled craft. And had obviously lain there for many days. The bodies were scattered where they had been butchered. The stench of decay was sickening, and the sight was horrible. The seagulls were scavengers of the dead. That was why the ship had attracted the birds. Everything was dappled white with the gulls' droppings, adding to the nauseating reek of decay. I felt my gorge rise but fought it down. I wouldn't be sick, not now, not here.

"Fan out, men," commanded Captain Hunter. "Check her from stem to stern. If anyone's alive in this charnel house, we must rescue them or give up our hope of heaven!"

With muttered "Ayes" the crew members began to move out across the gore-splattered decks. They were quiet and effective, but even those hardened men avoided looking at the dead. Uncle Patch called out. I thought he was examining a body, but he had made another sort of discovery.

"Don't know about the other two, William," he said, pointing at the stub of the mainmast, "but this mast was chopped down with an ax. Bad luck it didn't hole the hull when it crashed and take whoever did this with it!"

"Guns are gone," I blurted. Uncle Patch and Captain Hunter turned toward me, and in the heat and stink of decay, once again I almost threw up. But I didn't. "You can see where they used to be, the scars where they ran out and back, but they're gone!"

"Twelve pounders, judging by the shot that's left," Hunter said. "And six cannons, judging by the ports cut in her side."

"What kind of loon tries to move twelve pounders from ship to ship in the middle of the sea?" wondered Uncle Patch. "A false move, a snapped line, and a heavy cannon could punch right through the decks and down through the bottom of the ship."

"Could they have shoved the guns over the side?" I asked, just to show I was still paying attention, and to keep my mind off my heaving stomach.

"Could have, but why?" Hunter replied. "I mean, the ship's abandoned, a derelict. If you wanted the guns gone, why not just sink the whole bloody bark and be done with it?"

"Cap'n!" called the voice of Mr. Conway from up on the quarterdeck. "Ye need to attend here!"

"What is it, Mr. Conway?"

"Sorry, sir. 'Fraid ye need t' see this for yerself!"

"Blood and blast," snapped my uncle. "Now it's mysteries we're having. As if anything could be worse than this floating tomb!"

Up we went, me hurrying along behind. Mr. Conway moved aside and we saw what he had summoned us to see. For the second time since boarding the *Elizabeth Bingham* we all stood speechless.

The captain of the derelict bark lay on the desk. He had been slashed with a sword and sprawled there on his back, dead and past hope. A pistol rested near his outflung right hand, showing that he had died trying to defend himself and his vessel. The man lay with his head slightly propped against the bulkhead. And hanging from a cord around his neck was a sheet of stiff parchment on which someone had carefully lettered the message:

SO DIE ALL ROBBED BY MAD WILLIAM HUNTER!

The only sounds were the complaints of the remaining gulls and the hushed voices of our boarding party, calling out to one another.

There were too many dead to bury them properly, so Captain Hunter instead ordered the sea cocks opened. It took a lot of work since the derelict was practically swamped with water. One of the men dropped into the main hold, though, landing in water that went up to his armpits. He ducked under to find the lever. Finally he succeeded, letting seawater flood into her holds. He came scrambling out, shivering, and we rowed back to the *Aurora* to watch the other craft settle herself lower and lower into the water. The seaman who had dived into the hold muttered that he had the stink of death upon him from the water in the *Elizabeth Bingham,* and he dipped into the ocean to wash it off before he came up the side.

"Thank you," Captain Hunter told the man as he gave him a hand up onto the deck. I think we were all grateful that he had let the water into the bark. The only other choice would have been to fire our cannons at her, and that seemed cruel after all she had gone through.

So in the end, we stood off and watched the bark and her crew slip with a sort of crippled grace beneath the sea. The last thing I saw of her was the gleam of the gold lettering on her stern.

And then even that was gone.

CHAPTER 2

The Mystery

HARDLY HAD THE WATERS closed over the *Elizabeth Bingham* and her ghastly crew of dead men before Captain Hunter and my uncle left the deck. I followed them into the cabin of the *Aurora*. Captain Hunter sat at his table, and my uncle sat on the lockers under the stern windows, leaning back and interlacing his fingers across his chest. The light streaming through the great stern windows glinted in his copper-red hair. "Someone does not like you, William," he observed mildly.

Captain Hunter shook his head, making his blond queue sway back and forth. I shrank into the chair in the corner, drawing up my knees and keeping as still as any mouse, for far too often the two of them chased me out just when their talk became most interesting.

From where I sat, I could see the parchment that had hung around the neck of the unfortunate captain of the *Elizabeth Bingham.* It lay on Captain Hunter's table. He tapped it thoughtfully with his long fingers. "Well, Patch," he said, "we have enemies enough, Lord knows. After we broke from prison in Port Royal, every honest sailor's hand was against us. And after we and Don Esteban worked together to smash Jack Steele's armada at Tortuga, a number of pirates have decided we are enemies."

"Aye," Uncle Patch said tartly. "But would any sailor, honest or crooked, leave such a message for Lord knows who to find? 'Tis clear to me that someone is working at cross-purposes with us. For very close to a year now you have been making yourself known as a pirate—friendly to British buccaneers but hostile to the Spanish. Now, this was an English ship, and a brutal set of murders. Not even the Brotherhood of the Coast would wish to do business with the bloodthirsty fiend that the note implies you are."

I slipped out from my chair and came to stand behind the captain. Something about the note had caught my attention. "Captain Hunter," I said suddenly, "there is something very strange about this note."

"Strange indeed, and wicked," grumbled the captain. "It has been penned by some modern-day Ananias, for it is a lie from first to last."

"No, sir." I reached out to pick up the piece of parchment. "There is only one letter *S* in the entire message."

Captain Hunter read through the words. "Why, so there is, Davy, but what has that to do with the price of fish?"

I handed the parchment back to him. "It is also the only letter of the message written in red ink."

My uncle gave a sudden creak, the closest he ever approached to a laugh. "Look closer, nephew. 'Tis red, sure enough, but it is not ink."

I felt my skin crawl as I realized the brownish-red letter had been written with a pen dipped in blood. Swallowing my horror, I said, "What if the note is meant to let the reader guess about the real murderer? What if the man who really killed all those sailors has left us his initial?"

Captain Hunter was smiling, but without any real trace of amusement. "*S* is for Steele."

My uncle creaked again, and he suddenly broke into a childish singsong:

"*P* is for pirate, who's up to no good;

"*Q* is for *Red Queen,* the color of blood;

"*R* is for rogue, a murdering cad;

"*S* is for Steele, the worst of the bad!"

With a chuckle, Captain Hunter said, "You have unexpected talents, Doctor."

"Sure, I shall set up to be a poet," returned my uncle. "I shall go to live in Grub Street in London Town, and stain my fingers with ink and stuff my pockets with air, for that's all the payment most poets receive for their scribbling!"

I had to laugh at the thought of my hulking uncle becoming a poet, for in truth he looked to be the most dangerous man aboard the ship— broad-shouldered, tall, and muscular. It had taken me months to learn that this explosive man could be a good uncle, and a good friend. "It has to be Steele," I said.

My uncle raised an eyebrow. "Did I say ye nay? You have a good eye, Davy, and a quick mind. I'm positive you are right. Our pretending to be pirates will not fool Jack Steele. He knows you are searching for him, William, and this is his way of throwing stumbling blocks into your path."

Captain Hunter waved the note. "I am not so certain that we ourselves were not intended to find this parchment. Steele knows what waters we have been sailing. It would be just like that villain to want to sign his bloody work. His mind is twisted and bent like a corkscrew—"

"A rusty one," Uncle Patch put in. "Aye, but sharp as a new needle for all that. Well, William, and what are we to do about this? So far the English have not seriously hunted us, for we have disturbed mostly Spanish privateers. But if this sort of word gets abroad, you may be sure that even Sir Henry Morgan will not be able to keep the Royal Navy in check."

When the captain did not immediately reply, I said, "Much would depend on how fast this word gets about. How many ships has Steele taken? And how many of them are English? And on how many of them has he left such a calling card?"

"All good questions, Davy," said Captain Hunter. "But ones we cannot answer, not while we are at sea."

"They *do* need to be answered, though," Uncle Patch said. "How far has the word spread about you? We need to solve that mystery, and soon. Otherwise we shall find ourselves fleeing from every larger ship we meet."

The captain put both of his hands flat upon the table. "There is only one thing for it. We must look in on Port Royal. That's the center of news in these parts, and there we shall learn what Steele is up to with these tricks of his."

Uncle Patch snorted. "And are we to sail boldly in beneath the guns of Fort Morgan and Fort Charles, then? As I recall, they tried their best to sink us when last we were in Port Royal Harbor. They may have better luck if you give them a second chance!"

"Of course we cannot take the *Aurora* in," the captain acknowledged evenly. "It would be foolhardy even to try, and I am not about to put the lives of my men at such risk. But where a whole ship could not peep into Port Royal Harbor, a small fishing craft would have no trouble. Particularly if it were manned by a youngster."

"No!" My uncle's face flamed a brilliant crimson. "I smoke what you intend, William, and I tell you flat, the answer is no! My nephew is no more to be put at risk than your sailors!"

"I can do it," I insisted, for I, too, had caught Captain Hunter's drift.

Green eyes flashed at me. "This has nothing to do with you!"

"It has everything to do with me," I told Uncle Patch. "Am I not a member of the crew? I eat the same rations as they, and I do my job aboard ship, the same as they. And the captain is right. When we lived in Port Royal, I saw all manner of boys and men set out a-fishing at all hours of the day and night. 'Twould be easy for me to hang some nets over the bows of one of the gigs and sail her in amongst the other fishers."

"Exactly," Captain Hunter said. "Doctor, there really is no question about it. Of all aboard, Davy is the one likeliest to slip in and out of port without being noticed. Descriptions of us are out, but

I'd stake my wig that no one here would know Davy. His hair is longer than it was, and the sea air has bleached it lighter. He's grown nigh a foot, and his skin is brown with the sun. He's not at all the pasty twelve-year-old anyone in Port Royal would remember!"

They quarreled far into the afternoon, with the captain urging the sensibility of his plan and my uncle steadfastly condemning it as an idiotic way to get me shot. That day ended with no resolution, but I knew that, by and by, Uncle Patch would come around to the captain's way of thinking. As the captain reminded him, Uncle Patch was the one who had insisted that solving the mystery and learning something of Steele's movements was so important. Uncle Patch hated having his own words used against him, and he swore that he would never consent to such a plot. But I knew them both well, and from that moment onward, I planned to go ashore in Port Royal.

The next morning the question was still unsettled. Uncle Patch and I had the usual sick call, but by and large, the *Aurora* had a healthy crew. I think the men were kept that way by the constant exercise of sailing

PIRATE HUNTER

the ship, together with their diet, for Uncle Patch was scrupulous about taking on fresh food at out-of-the-way harbors and anchorages. Never were the men without greenstuff and salt meat that was less than a year old. Even the ship's bread was fresher than the hard tack of the Royal Navy, and mostly free of the weevils and maggots that crawled in the king's bread.

However it fell out, we had not even one patient that day, so I was free until lessons began after noon. I went onto a strangely busy deck. "Watch your step, Davy!" shouted Mr. Jeffers. He knelt on the deck, and I noticed again how his left ear was strangely crumpled after having been sliced to ribbons by a flying splinter and sewn up again by my uncle.

Now Mr. Jeffers rose to his feet and stood over a long strip of canvas, three feet wide and stretching the whole length of the deck. Six sailors were slapping paint over it, sky-blue paint, but were being mindful not to splatter any upon the precious deck. "What is this, Mr. Jeffers?" I asked, carefully stepping over the corner of the canvas.

"'Tis a sort of disguise, ye might say," responded

24

Mr. Jeffers with a low, gurgling chuckle. "Want to help, lad?"

Soon enough I had a paintbrush in my hand and my own section of canvas to paint. Work went rapidly, and as soon as the canvas was painted, the sailors hauled it up and hung it out to dry. The deck had been fouled after all, but the men hurried to correct that with turpentine and the flat grinding stones they called bibles. Soon they had rubbed out all traces of paint.

Meanwhile, a work party had lowered platforms from the larboard bows. Men sitting on these began to repaint the sides of the *Aurora*, making the black-and-yellow hull the same sky blue as the canvas we had painted. Mr. Jeffers enjoyed my puzzlement, and he steadfastly refused to explain anything to me.

My uncle conducted lessons that afternoon, as he always did. I was coming along well in anatomy and in the compounding of medicines. I was even becoming tolerably good at writing, and some of the books my uncle made me read were passably interesting. Mr. Adams joined us later in the afternoon watch for mathematics, for he had been a midshipman in the Royal Navy before we began to masquerade as pirates. He would never achieve his heart's desire—becoming a full lieutenant—without mastering the mathematics of navigation. Mr. Adams had long believed himself too stupid to learn trigonometry and angles and all the rest. Lord knows my uncle was the worst teacher in the world for all this, for he had barely a grasp of multiplication beyond five times nine.

Yet he was so willing to teach, and he had so many books to teach from, that Mr. Adams applied himself with a will and had begun to understand much more than he had ever believed he could. Indeed, my uncle himself was picking up more and more mathematics as we went along, and though I felt myself dull when trying to make out some of the problems, even I had begun to clutch at a few concepts.

The last lesson for me was Latin, and Mr. Adams left us then. By the time we had finished with Cicero that day, it was nearly eight bells, or four o'clock in landsman's terms. I emerged blinking from the cabin and walked into the smell of paint and turpentine. The change in the frigate's appearance amazed me. One side of her was now a sunny blue, and the other side was beginning to get the same treatment. Our figurehead, a bosomy woman holding a torch and representing Aurora, the pagan goddess of the dawn, lay in the bows, stretched out and lifting her torch as if pleading for someone to give her a hand up.

Aloft, sailors were creeping through the rigging and gingerly handling the foretopgallant mast, which they had taken from its seat and were lowering on lines to the deck. All of this was a puzzle to me.

Mr. Jeffers and his crew had unfurled the strips of blue canvas, for there were two of them now, not one, and both had more or less dried in the hard glare of the tropical sun. Now his men were busily painting black squares on the blue canvas.

"Gunports!" I yelled, suddenly understanding what the squares were supposed to represent. "You're painting false gunports on the canvas! But why?" I meant that we had real gunports. The *Aurora* was a frigate, a narrow, sleek, French-built ship, with almost all her cannons ranged on both sides of the main deck.

Mr. Jeffers laughed. He had a long smudge of black paint across his nose. "'Tis a merchantman's trick, young Davy. To make a pirate or any enemy think she's got teeth, a merchantman will paint false gunports along her side."

"But we have twenty-eight real cannons!"

"Aye, so we have." Mr. Jeffers dipped his brush into a pot of black paint and began to make the edge of his false gun port a little uneven.

Then I realized they were all uneven. Some were six inches too high, some six inches too low. They were not all one size, either. At a distance, they might fool another ship, but if one came within telescope range, it would be obvious that these were poor imitations.

Perhaps the figurehead of Aurora shed some light into my thick skull at that moment. "You want people to think we're just a disguised merchantman!" I exclaimed.

A hand clapped my shoulder. It belonged to Captain Hunter, who looked strange in a smock-shirt and gray pantaloons, both of them daubed and smeared with blue and black paint. "Just so, Davy," he said with a laugh. "As soon as our last coat of blue paint is dry on the transom, a couple of fellows will paint our new name there: the *Fairweather*. We will lose our fine towering masts and instead show the world the stumpy sticks of a trading ship. To all the world we will be a British merchant ship out of, oh, say, Edinburgh. It won't be a thorough enough disguise to let us into Port Royal Harbor, but I reckon we can fool most vessels we meet."

Over the next four days I came to believe that Captain Hunter was right. In fact, I was not sure that we would not be able to sail into Port Royal, or into any harbor in the West Indies, without being known for what we were. Once the topgallant masts were all struck, the figurehead stowed, and the ship transformed into a sky-blue beauty, the false gunports were tacked to the side, neatly covering the real ports. In an emergency it would be the work of a moment to rip the canvas away, or even to fire right through it. Yet, from a distance the illusion was wonderful.

I learned that when I rowed Captain Hunter and my uncle one-half mile away to admire the new look. With her shorter masts and her new paint, the *Aurora* seemed somehow fatter and slower than she really was. Captain Hunter had ordered the oldest, grayest sails to be run up, too. There was nothing of naval smartness about our poor ship now.

To add to the deception, the captain had ordered the decks to be cluttered with barrels and boxes. A small pyramid of these stood amidships, covered with a tarpaulin and lashed down. Anyone would have sworn we were an innocent ship, somewhat slovenly, loaded to the scuppers with trade goods.

"The paint don't go all the way to the water," observed my uncle critically. "There's still a dark rim."

"It makes no great odds," Captain Hunter declared. "A ship's always dirty right around the waterline, from the slush and muck heaved overboard. Anyway, we cannot careen her out of the water and do a proper job of painting her right down to the copper. This will do. If anyone comes near enough to spy the black paint, we've let him come too close, anyway!"

Uncle Patch still shook his head, as if unsatisfied. "We've far too many men for a merchant vessel. What are our numbers? One hundred and sixty?"

"One hundred and fifty-seven," Captain Hunter said softly.

I wondered if he was thinking of the men we had lost in battles and through illness, for that was what I was thinking. We had begun our cruise with some two hundred men.

"Far too many," grumbled my uncle. "I have never known a merchant ship to have more than a couple of dozen."

"I see no problem there," Captain Hunter said easily. "We sail with the full crew when we are out of sight of land or other vessels, and when we are closer in, most of the men will hide belowdecks. Mr. Adams can appear as the master of the vessel, perhaps wearing my court wig and with a pillow stuffed into his shirt to give him the proper fat-merchant look."

"For of course you are too well-known to show yourself," Uncle Patch said sarcastically.

"Row us back, Davy," said the captain. To my uncle he said very seriously, "I just may be too well-known, Patch. For I have the feeling that Steele, devil that he is, has done his foul work all too well."

It seemed I was ever and again learning new things about Uncle Patch. One calm evening the captain told the crew to be lazy and enjoy the fair weather, so hard had they worked at transforming the ship. At sunset they gathered in the forward part of the main deck and sat or lay back listening to Lloyd Jones scrape at his fiddle. Jones, a stringy, lean man of forty or so, was scratching out a mournful tune, suited almost to a funeral.

I sat leaning against the mainmast, listening with the rest. Uncle Patch came on deck, sniffed the air, and then walked to the windward rail, where he stood staring out over the sea. Presently he turned and in a chiding voice said, "Jones, the Lord commanded us to make a joyful noise, not a doleful Welsh whine. Play something cheerful!"

Jones coughed and said, "Well, maybe I would if Your Honor would consent to lead us in a song."

I almost laughed aloud at the very thought of my grumbling uncle bursting into melody, but he chuckled and said, "Fairly spoken! Very well. D'ye know 'Fare thee well, my darlin' Kathleen?'"

"Spin it out, and I'll follow," responded Jones.

To my surprise and considerable embarrassment, my uncle planted his feet, put one hand on his chest, and broke out in a clear, strong tenor:

Fare thee well, my darlin' Kathleen,
A thousand times adieu,
I am bound, I am bound from Dublin Town
And the girl I love so true.
I will sail the salt seas over,
Ten thousand miles or more,
But I'll return to the girl I love
And Dublin Town once more—

He paused, and the whole crew stamped or slapped the deck and roared, "Fine girl you are!" by way of refrain. Jones had picked up the lively tune at once and jigged it out on his fiddle. My uncle took up the song again:

You're the girl that I adore,
And still I live in hopes to see
Old Dublin Town once more!

That was the chorus, and as he sang his way through the song, the men always introduced it with their lusty cry of "Fine girl you are!"

Of all the words, I remember only one more
verse he sang, an ill-omened one:

And now the storm is ragin',
And we are far from shore,
The sheets and lines are stretched
and wrung,
And the riggin' is all tore. . . .

There, I forget the rest. But I do recall that Uncle
Patch finished his warbling to shouts of approval. I
was glad that twilight had come, for to me his
behavior was so unlike him that it made my heart
heavy to think on him making a fool of himself that
way, and I know my face was a-burning red.

And besides, besides, besides . . .

My dead mother's name was Kathleen.

CHAPTER 3

I Go A-spying

HOW WELL JACK STEELE had done his work was made known to us only two days later. It was but a bit after noon when we spotted a sail away to the west. Immediately, Captain Hunter gave the order and most of the men disappeared below-decks. This would be the first test of our new disguise.

"Are you feeling like a proper captain, Mr. Adams?" Captain Hunter said, adjusting his good black court wig, which now resided atop the first mate's head.

"Begging your pardon, sir, but what I most feel like is a proper fool." Mr. Adams stood patiently as the captain yanked at the wig again. Mr. Adams was dressed in a blue uniform jacket from the stores, a white blouse and breeches, and a perfectly respectable hat. The only problem was that none of his new finery exactly fit.

"Be glad we talked him out of the pillow, lad," creaked Uncle Patch, "or you'd be looking like a fat fool on top of it."

"None of you have any sense of the theatrical," the captain sighed, finally finished manhandling the wig on poor Mr. Adams's head.

"Perhaps I'll grow into it, sir."

"Close in on her, Mr. Warburton," Captain Hunter called up to our helmsman. "Let's see what's going on in the wide world!"

"Aye," muttered my uncle. "And what kind of role we're playing in it."

Over the next hour, we slowly closed in on the other vessel. It soon became clear that she was a sharp-looking sloop, sleek and well maintained, and like ourselves, stacked high with boxes and barrels. She was also armed with a brace of twelve pounders on each side. As we got closer, I could see men suspiciously crouched over those guns, slow matches at the ready. A tall, slim man with auburn hair tied back in a queue stood at the stern and stared back at us.

"All right, Mr. Adams," whispered Captain Hunter from where he lounged on the railing next to him. "Do your duty, sir."

Mr. Adams squared his shoulders and brought his speaking trumpet to his lips. "Ahoy the sloop! What ship are you?"

The man with the auburn queue stared at us for a moment, then raised his own trumpet. "This be the *Piedmont Star* out of Charles Town, bound for Antigua, George Edwards, captain. What ship are you?"

"This be the *Fairweather* out of Edinburgh, bound for Port Royal. I am Captain Adams."

The man on the sloop bawled, "Port Royal? Then hoist all yer sails and come about, *Fairweather,* for ye be sailing into rough waters!"

"Rough waters?" Mr. Adams called. "Mean you storms, Captain Edwards?"

"Has Scotland broke loose and drifted out to sea that you get no news, Captain Adams? I mean pirates! Mad William Hunter prowls the waters around Port Royal!"

Captain Hunter jerked up at the sound of his name but then caught control of himself and, with a nod of his head, instructed Mr. Adams to carry on. Our first mate looked nervous as he raised his trumpet again.

"Mad William Hunter? But we fly the Union flag and he never attacks British ships!"

"Tell that to the crews of the *Lord Marlborough* and the *Princess of Wales*—if only you can find them. Beware a black-and-yellow French frigate— that be the wicked *Aurora* herself. Show her your heels, and may the devil take the dog!"

And with that, the *Piedmont Star* pulled away from us and headed off on her way. No one, not even Uncle Patch, said a word, but all eyes turned to where Captain Hunter leaned back against the railing.

"Well, that does answer the question of whether Steele has taken other English ships," he said at last.

"Aye," grumbled Uncle Patch. "And whether or not our reputation has suffered in the bargain."

Captain Hunter smiled at him, but somehow the smile never quite reached his eyes.

We hailed several other ships but received no more useful news. At last we stood off south of Port Royal.

The time was hours before dawn, and I waited on deck, receiving my orders from Uncle Patch.

"The plan is simple, so see that ye hold to it, lad!" he said, staring me straight in the eyes with never a blink. "You're to head ashore in the skiff alongside. We're to continue westward to a quiet anchorage William knows of. You have one week from today to get your snooping done. After that, every night at midnight, we'll stand off here until three o'clock. Understand? Three o'clock and not a moment past!"

I nodded earnestly, it being at least the fourth time he had told me, then shocked him by giving him a great hug. Before he could do anything more than sputter, I was over the side and into the skiff. Then it was only a matter of seconds before I was loose from the *Aurora* and rowing for all I was worth toward Port Royal.

The night was dark, but the sky was rich with stars and a late moon was was low in the west. I could see the faint harbor lights in the distance. I started to find the rhythm of rowing, putting my back into the effort. Ten or fifteen minutes passed.

"Any luck, lad?"

The voice to my starboard nearly made me swallow my tongue. I stared wildly into the night and could just barely make out another small fishing boat with two men in it. One was chuckling softly to himself. At last it came to me that they were only asking about the fishing. Relief washed over me like a tumbling wave.

"Not a single fish did I have for a night's work!" I called. "And yourselves?"

"'Twas not a total waste o' time. Next time go a bit north. The fish there know how to help a poor man earn a penny!"

They laughed again and I with them. They were fishermen, as I was supposed to be. My luck had held true. Around me in the dark I could now see other small boats heading back into Port Royal. Once I was sure of my heading, I risked hoisting the skiff's small sail so that I could give my weary arms a rest. The wind was only indifferent, but with a careful hand at the tiller and on the lines, I steered for the harbor.

Around me other voices drifted back and forth, complaining and joking about their luck, good or bad. I was just another poor soul trying to make a little extra money. Just as Captain Hunter had planned.

The sun was slowly starting to rise when I tied up my skiff in the shelter of a lonely dock. Other boats bobbed beside it, enough to keep it safe for the time being. It wasn't the kind of craft anyone would want to steal, anyway, being old, gray, and splintered. Just about any other vessel would be more tempting to a thief.

Port Royal had changed not a whit since I had landed on these same docks more than a year earlier. Everywhere there was a bustle and crowds hurrying back and forth. For the first few moments I walked in fear, certain that any moment someone would point at me and shout, "There he is! There's that famous pirate, Davy Shea!" Then, of course, I remembered that I had never been the famous pirate Davy Shea or even the famous loblolly boy Davy Shea. I was just another ragged boy making his way in the world. I walked a bit more jauntily after that.

At last I made my way to the good old King's Mercy, where my uncle and I had lived before all this excitement had begun. Strangely enough, it too still looked the same. Surely it should have changed. After all, I certainly had. I pushed open the stout old oaken door and walked into the dimly lit great room. A robust figure in a long dress was bustling around the tables. I walked up to her with my hat in my hands.

"Beg pardon, Mrs. Cochran, but my uncle bids me to remind you that he still wishes you to keep his room ready for him. He asked me to give you this"— here I fished a small bag of golden coins from my shirt—"and says he trusts that all is in order."

Mrs. Molly Cochran, the most levelheaded and straightforward woman I had ever met, turned and stared at me.

Then she screamed.

Some time later, she hovered over me with a scolding tongue. "Davy Shea, ten years you took off my life with your foolishness! Eat; you look like your own ghost, you do!"

I nodded apologetically and stuffed another half rasher of bacon into my mouth. After she finished yelling at me for being an inconsiderate rascal, Mrs. Cochran insisted on making enough breakfast for me and at least three other boys. Fortunately they hadn't shown up.

"I'm so sorry, ma'am, I wasn't thinking. . . ."

"Like your uncle you are—sets a goal, heads for it, and Lord help anything in his way. Is he himself well?"

"Was when I left, ma'am. More eggs, please?"

"What? Oh, yes, eat up." She dished another mound of scrambled eggs onto my platter with a look of pleasure on her face. In truth, she was about the best cook I had ever run across, and even a homely dish of scrambled eggs tasted the better for her touch. She beamed as I began to eat, and said, "You just missed Jessie and dear Miss Fairfax. . . ."

I almost choked. "I thought Jessie and Helena, uh, Miss Fairfax had returned to England?" Jessie was Mrs. Cochran's daughter. She was a brown-eyed, brown-haired girl a little older than I was. The best I can say of her is that she tended to make life interesting everywhere she went. For that matter, so did Miss Helena Fairfax.

"No, bless you, the lady is living at her great-uncle's house in Spanish Town. That would be Sir Reginald Fairfax who sits on the council—frankly, because Governor Molesworth had to put him someplace."

"Beg pardon?"

"Sir Reginald has lived in Jamaica in perpetual disgrace for as long as anyone can remember. He's the living definition of an old rake, he is, and thrilled to have someone as respectable as his grandniece to run his establishment for him. Quality folks are calling on him that haven't set foot in that house for thirty years. Or so I'm told, since I'm not a gossiping woman like some I could name. . . ."

Mrs. Cochran rattled on like that until I was through with all the eggs and bacon and had sopped up what was left with half a loaf of fresh-baked bread. Finally, stuffed full as a Christmas goose, I asked the question I had been sent here by Captain Hunter to ask.

"Beg pardon, Mrs. Cochran, but I've been sent back with a mission to complete. I have to learn what the feelings are toward Captain Hunter and the rest of us that sail on the *Aurora*. What do they think of us here in Port Royal?"

Mrs. Cochran sat there in silence for a moment, her lips pressed together in a tight little line. Even before she finally spoke, I knew the news would not be to our liking.

"I'll not lie to you, Davy Shea. It's not good, not good at all. In fact, it's as bad as it can be. At least two English ships have been found plundered and left as derelicts."

"Aye, the *Lord Marlborough* and the *Princess of Wales*."

"True, but there are others that have not reached port. They now are weeks overdue. And there were . . . *things* found on the derelicts that point straight and true at William Hunter and your uncle. Things were done to, well, to the bodies of some of the dead . . . and . . . and there were . . . there were . . ."

I finished her thought: "There were messages and signs that plainly said 'Mad William Hunter.'"

She sat back and stared at me. "If you know the answers, Davy, why are you asking the questions?"

I told her about the *Elizabeth Bingham* and what we had discovered on board her before we had sent her to the bottom of the sea. She nodded sadly. "That's the rumor we have had swirling around Port Royal for the past weeks. And you are telling me on your honor as a Christian that there is not a short ounce of truth to them?"

"On my honor and hope for salvation, Mrs. Cochran, we had nothing to do with those horrors!"

"Then that's enough for me." She smiled. "Not that I could've believed it to begin with. Folk don't change like that. I've had your uncle here in this house off and on for more than five years and William close unto death in it for more than five months. And my Jessie can no more keep a secret than she can flap her arms and fly to the moon. I know what the lot of you are doing out there and it has nothing to do with slaughtering fellow Englishmen, and that's the end of it!"

And with that final stern statement of support, I was hustled up the stairs to our old rooms and told to go to bed before I dropped off from exhaustion. Stuffed full of a good English breakfast and tired beyond belief, I tumbled into my own bed and was dead to the world in a manner of moments, no matter how much sunlight came streaming in through the dormer window.

"Only a mooncalf would go to bed at dawn and wake at dusk!"

That argumentative voice met me with full force as I staggered back down the stairs later that day. At the foot of the stairs, hands planted on her hips, was Jessie Cochran staring up at me. In a world of constant change, she alone seemed to stay the same.

"Hello, Jessie," I said with a great yawn. I had just reached the foot of the stairs when I was caught up in a strong hug that took my very breath away.

"Oh, Davy, it is so good to see you alive and well!"

Miss Helena Fairfax, who had spent most of our acquaintance disguised as a British naval officer, was much different as a woman. For some reason she seemed smaller and smelled . . . different. Mrs. Cochran smelled of baking and good hard English soaps. Miss Fairfax smelled of exotic flowers and vanilla and clean red hair.

"Hello," I said as she let go of me. Jessie was glaring at me, so I judged it wise to add no more than that.

"Dear Mrs. Cochran has told us of your mission. I know that it is most important. I spent some time with Captain William Hunter, and I know he is not capable of the horrible crimes attributed to him!"

Her cheeks had turned very pink, and her eyes flashed. I stammered, "Th-thank you, miss, it would make him feel good to hear it."

"It would? Really? How delightful. Still, that does not change the fact that nearly everyone else considers him the most feared and hated freebooter in the West Indies. Captain Steele seems to have been quite successful in that."

"Yes, miss. That's why I plan to spend my time roaming the streets in hopes of hearing more of these cruel rumors."

"Why would you do that?" demanded Jessie. "You know what they are saying out there! How many times do you have to hear it? That's not what's important, you mooncalf!"

I gave her a cold look. "Oh, and it's a better idea you'd be having, Jessie Cochran?"

"I'd be hard pressed not to! Why go wandering the streets when all of Port Royal now comes to the King's Mercy?"

For a second or two, I stood blinking at her. "But I thought no one came to the King's Mercy because pirates had stayed here!"

"That was before you became famous bloodthirsty

pirate murderers! Now everyone has to come and have a drink in the famous King's Mercy!"

"'Tis true," said her mother in a guilty voice. "Business has been rather brisk of late."

Miss Fairfax was tapping a finger on her chin. "That is a clever idea, Jessie."

Jessie beamed at her.

Then Miss Fairfax turned her startling eyes on me. "I would strongly suggest that you abandon your idea of wandering the city, Davy, and instead settle yourself here to gather information for the good Captain Hunter."

"As opposed to the one everybody's talking about," muttered Jessie.

I sighed, for I know when I'm outgunned and outmaneuvered. They were right, and arguing would not change that. So that afternoon I started to help Mrs. Cochran as her new potboy, running back and forth with food and drink for the guests and boarders of King's Mercy. No one would notice me, for people never notice the folks who wait on them. I would run and fetch and go.

And listen.

CHAPTER 4

The Drunkard's Tale

I SWEAR, HAD I known that my spying would take the form of being a servant at the beck and call of every rough customer who tottered in the door of the King's Mercy, I would have had second thoughts. For days I ran my legs to stubs, fetching and carrying. Through it all, for my pains I got mainly curses and abuse, though at an odd time a sailor would toss a halfpenny piece my way. It was a small enough reward.

But to top off my misery, Jessie Cochran had come to stay with her mother for a spell while Miss Fairfax was away visiting her cousins in Port Maria, away on the north shore of Jamaica. Now that girl had ways of tormenting me that her mother would never dream of. Somehow she had yet to forgive me for having shown up months and months before at the front door, alone, orphaned, and friendless.

On that occasion she had flung a basin of dirty water squarely into my face and had called me a thief and a runagate. Never mind that from the pity in my heart I had taught her to read, or that I had rescued her from captivity on the island of Tortuga. To be sure, I did have my uncle's help in the rescue, and some from Captain Hunter as well, but to hear Jessie tell it, you would have thought she had planned the whole thing herself and that our coming with the very ship she had sailed away on was just part of her scheme.

Be that as it may, as the owner's daughter, she naturally outranked a mere potboy, and so she was forever ordering me to do this or that, to scrape and wash dishes, to mind the fire, to chop stove wood, to run to the market for more molasses, for four good fat chickens, for this or for that or for the other. Pillar to post it was, so that by the third day I began to dread the sun's peeping in my window, for it brought with it sixteen hours of harder work than I had ever known aboard ship.

And the devil a word did I hear of Steele. Drunken sailors babble and yarn, much to Mrs. Cochran's disgust, but none of them babbled of Steele or told stories of his whereabouts. They did speak now and again of Captain Hunter. For months after our escape from Port Royal, the King's Mercy had suffered, for the honest sailors avoided the place where the notorious doctor-pirate Patrick Shea had lived.

But somehow that had worn off with the passing of time, and now the drinkers at Molly Cochran's tables seemed rather proud of the place's reputation. "Aye," one sailor had roared the first night I was waiting tables, "Bill Hunter's a man, so he is! Snatched a neat sloop from under the guns of the fort, got clean away, and sinks Spaniards by the shipload! A health to him, says I!" No one joined in the toast, but I saw several men nod at the words.

As the days and nights passed, I began to despair of learning any real news. On my trips to market, or whenever I could get away from the King's Mercy for half an hour all together, I kept my ears open. For all I could tell, though, Steele had not yet left enough derelicts with his vicious calling cards on them to make a very terrible impression at Port Royal. Nor did it seem likely that I would fulfill the second part of my mission and learn something of the hiding places that Steele might have in this part of the world.

Finally, though, my luck changed on the unluckiest day of the week for sailors—a Friday. That was the first night that I was to sail out and rendezvous with the *Aurora,* at midnight. Long before then, however, a stumbling, grizzled old sailor blundered into the King's Mercy, squalling for rum.

He was bald on top, with a long, unkempt fringe of iron-gray hair. His face was all scarred and battered, his nose so broken that the tip of it almost touched his lower lip. He wore no shoes, pantaloons that might once have been blue, and a raggedy calico shirt with a blue-and-white pattern. He had lost all his teeth in front, and he spoke in a hoarse, mumbling roar. "Rum! Rum here for a sailor man! Be quick about it!"

I got him seated, and it was then that I noticed all the tattoos on his sinewy arms. Mermaids and spouting whales, compass roses and anchors crowded the flesh, most of them sun-faded and ancient. But on the back of his right hand, where it must have hurt like blazes as it was being done, was a laughing skull above two crossed cutlasses, picked out in red. It looked more recent than the others.

And the image was the same as the one that Jack Steele flew on his bloodred pirate flag.

As I drew a measure of rum, I told Mrs. Cochran that this might be the very man who could answer at least some of our questions, and I begged her to let me hover in his corner as much as I could. She agreed, but warned, "He's a rough-looking customer, Davy. Be ye careful, hear?"

The old fellow drank the rum greedily and called for another. I brought him another measure, a double one, and when he had finished that, yet another. By then he was staring and snorting, and I felt bold enough to ask, "New in these waters, Captain?"

He glared at me with a bleared brown eye. "Shut your gob, cabin boy!" And he snatched the latest round of rum from me as if he feared I would take it away from him.

By and by he began to talk, in a muttering, grumbling undertone. He was not speaking to me, but to

himself, or perhaps to companions he only imagined to be sitting by his side. "Call 'emselves pirates.
These don't be pirates nowadays," he said in a thick
voice. "None of 'em is a patch on old Morgan.
Bunch of lily-livered landlubbers, the lot of 'em!"

You may be sure I kept the rum flowing, and I
hung about to hear as much as I could of his ram-
bling. The old man stared down at the glass in his
hands and talked to it. After a time, as I took away
one glass and set down a fresh one, I again spoke to
him. "They say Jack Steele's a man."

"Aye!" he snapped. "Steele! There's a right gentleman o' fortune for ye. Strong as a ox, mean as a
snake, that 'un. Sailed with 'im once on a time, did I."

Since he had not snapped my head off, I said in a
low voice, "I'd give a lot to run away and join him,
I would. This is no life for a lad of spirit."

He glared at me again. "You! You wouldn't last a
day on Steele's ship. Show me your hands, boy!"

I held out my hands, which were callused from
my climbing the rigging on the *Aurora*. He
grunted. "Well, well, so ye can do a day's work, at
that. But ain't no odds, boy. Join up with Steele,
says ye? No chance, says I. And for why? Ye can't

find old Steele, that's why! Nobody can, as he don't want anyone to find 'im."

"But you've sailed with him. Do you sail with him still?"

"Not I, laddie buck," the old fellow told me. "Nah, ol' Gaff is too broke of arm an' wind to climb the riggin' or point a cannon. Dismissed me, did Jack, with a bag o' gold an' not so much as a thank ye. But that's better nor what most o' my shipmates got, a knife in the back an' a berth in the ocean!"

He maundered on, going back to his youth in the north of England, where he was a minister's son, or so he claimed. Then he talked of taking prisoners at Barbados when Steele raided that island in 1682. Then he was off on some other thread of memory. I saw that he was going to pass out soon, so at half past nine I asked again where Jack Steele might be found.

"Anywhere," was his slurred response. "'E might be makin' the Pirates' Round and be off to Madagascar for the India trade. Or 'e might have sailed round the Horn an' be makin' 'is way to Panama." He hiccupped. "If 'e's off the Spanish Main, 'e's got a snug harbor at Bloodhaven. In these waters, maybe San . . ." His head reeled loosely on his neck.

"Santiago?" I asked, naming the principal port on the southeastern coast of Cuba.

"Nah, nah, San Angel. Tight little town, easy t' keep the Spaniards quiet, quiet, qui—" He pitched forward all of a sudden, his old head crashing onto the splintered table. In a flash, I was back in the kitchen, tugging at my apron.

Jessie, who stood at a tub full of soapy water and pewter dishes, scowled at me. "What are you about?"

"I've got to get to sea," I said, and in a few words I told her of what I had heard.

"San Angel?" asked Jessie, with a frown on her freckled face. "I've never heard of such a place, and I've lived here as long as I can remember. The man was drunk!"

"Drunk or sober, he's given me the first clue I've struck," I told her, and a moment later I was away.

A full moon was rising toward zenith, and in its light a good many small craft were gliding in the harbor. I got to my skiff, loosed the lines, and climbed in. A sentry on a wharf asked my business. "Fishing," I called back.

He was silent, and I rowed on until I fetched the harbor channel and ran up my single triangular sail. Again, I was not alone, for a good many of the working people of Port Royal went late-night fishing on nights with a good moon, and as one of a dozen or more small craft, my skiff was not easy to notice.

It was uncomfortable to sail, for even with the fair sky there was a storm stalking out on the sea somewhere, and it sent a choppy swell rolling through the darkness. I shipped some water and had to bail for a good while before getting the hang of it.

My navigation was nothing more than simple dead reckoning, but the wind favored me. I sailed out onto the dark ocean until Port Royal was only a smear of yellow light low on the horizon, and there I struck my sail and dropped my small anchor.

I lit my lantern and looked at my uncle's treasured silver pocketwatch. It was but ten minutes to eleven, and the *Aurora* would surely not show up before the set time. I had more than an hour to wait out on the open sea.

It was miserable, with the swell bobbing me up

and down like a cork in a millrace, and waves breaking over the bows at times, so that I had to bail again and again. Once two other fishing craft came toward me from the darkness, and I doused the lantern. They passed me by without even noticing me, calling to each other as they made wagers on how many fish they were going to take. Before long they were out of sight and out of earshot.

Then the devil's own time did I have striking another light, for my tinder was damp, but at long, long last I had the lantern alight again. By then it was nearly midnight, so I ran the lantern up the mast, where it hung pitching and bobbing. Looking at it made me feel seasick. I seem never to be bothered with that illness except when aboard a small craft.

I forced myself to look away and scan the dark horizon. Nothing. Time crept by like an aged beetle, and every minute seemed an hour.

If the watch had not told me that only twenty minutes had passed, I would have sworn that it was near dawn when I sighted the twin lights that had to be the *Aurora*. To make sure, I loosed the line that held my own lantern and lowered it and raised it again.

Sure enough, the top lanterns of the approaching vessel rose and then moved from side to side. Men at the masthead had seen my signal and were giving me the agreed answer. Now all I had to do was stay put until they got to me, but that was a wearisome business, for the wind that was fair to me was foul to them.

At long last, though, she hove to, and I rowed to her side and tied my skiff fast before climbing aboard. My uncle met me with, "What news?"

"Let me tell it all at once," I begged. "For I am weary, and I don't want to repeat it."

He and I joined Captain Hunter in the stern cabin, and there I poured out my story. "'Tis little enough, I know," I said as I finished the tale.

"It may be enough," said my uncle. "Bloodhaven, is it? And San Angel? William?"

In the light of the hanging cabin lantern, Captain Hunter went to the map chest and rummaged through its contents. He produced a chart and unrolled it atop his table. All three of us bent over it. "There is a San Angel in Mexico, I think, but that one's landlocked. Hardly the spot for a sea dog like Steele. But if I am not mistaken . . ."

His finger traced the southeastern tip of Cuba, drawn on the chart in a large scale. "I see it," said my uncle, stabbing his forefinger down at a spot well to the west of Santiago.

"Aye, just a fishing village of a few dozen souls," said Captain Hunter with a nod. "A narrow inlet, but uncommonly deep for these waters, and a rocky island just off the coast big enough to hide even a large vessel."

"Steele's hideout, then?" asked Uncle Patch.

"A rare place for smugglers, at any rate," returned Captain Hunter. "The Spaniards are forbidden by law to deal with any but their own ships. But the Spanish king charges such high prices for his goods that there's a brisk trade in stolen booty. San Angel is one of those quiet little corners that calls no attention to itself, but it's just the spot where, on a dark night, a British or French captain might quietly transfer a hold full of goods to an honest Spaniard's merchant ship—or the ship of a Spaniard who passes for honest, at any rate."

I was not to go back to the King's Mercy, it seemed. For that I was grateful, being worn out from my week of hard work and my night of rowing and sailing a cross-grained little skiff on that rolling sea. Straightaway I went belowdecks to my hammock, climbed in, and dropped into as deep a sleep as I have ever known.

The next morning we had cleared the eastern tip of Jamaica and were making our way north and west, toward San Angel. The wind almost failed us, and with the topsails set, we glided along at less than two knots. "It's just as well," said Captain Hunter, "for we must change our disguise."

He called for Mr. Grice, the sailmaker, and told him to make up all the flags appropriate to a Spanish trader. Then he had some men paint out the false name, *Fairweather,* that ran along the ship's transom. He walked the decks for more than an hour before exclaiming, "I have it!" He went to his cabin for a short space of time and came back with a sheet of paper on which he had hand-lettered *Cielo Claro*. He handed that to Mr. Tate, who was in charge of the painting crew. "This is to be our new name, Mr. Tate. Paint it on as fancy as you please."

"Dark blue and gilt?" asked Mr. Tate with a

gleam in his eye. He loved gold, even if it were only paint.

"Gilt, dark blue, whatever you wish," said Captain Hunter with a grin.

Uncle Patch peered over Mr. Tate's shoulder. "*Cielo Claro?*"

"We shall be the *Clear Sky*," answered the captain. "It's very close to *Fairweather*. Just the sort of unremarkable name that will draw no undue attention from the dons." He looked around. "Alonzo!"

A sailor in the mizzen top leaped from his perch as though he had lost his mind and was bent on dashing out his brains on the deck. He caught a stay, though, and slid down it, dropping off lightly and landing just before the captain. "Yes, sir?"

"How's your Spanish, Pedro Alonzo?" asked Captain Hunter.

Mr. Alonzo scratched his head. "Well, sir, I might be that bit rusty. I was brought up a-speakin' of it, but I've had small occasion to talk it since I was twelve or thereabout." I thought that Mr. Alonzo might now be three times that age. "What does your honor need?"

The captain grinned. "A ship's master, if a Spanish vessel hails us. Think you could tell 'em all that we're the *Cielo Claro,* fresh from Seville, if they ask?"

A relieved grin split Mr. Alonzo's dark, craggy face. "Oh, aye, that I can do with no trouble at all. I thought you wanted something more in the—the—litterarywary line."

"Just the talk of an honest Spanish merchant seaman, that's all," the captain assured him.

When Mr. Alonzo had left us to climb back to his post, Uncle Patch shook his head dolefully. "*Cielo Claro,* in faith! This will never answer, William. Any sailor with half an eye can see that the *Aurora* is French-built."

"Aye, but what of that?" Captain Hunter said carelessly. "I hope an honest Spanish merchant may buy his ship at any port he chooses. We'll get close enough to see whether the *Red Queen* is riding at anchor in the fairway to San Angel, you may rest assured of that."

"And then?" asked my uncle.

Captain Hunter shrugged. "One thing at a time, Doctor. First let us see whether this drunkard's tale of Jack Steele is just vaporings, or whether it has any sober truth at its bottom."

And not another word on the subject would he speak.

CHAPTER 5

Death and Desolation

IN THE DAYS that followed, we sailed along the southern coast of the great Spanish island possession of Cuba. Sparkling white beaches and mangrove swamps, lush forests and the distant mountains that formed the spine of the island slid past, broken only by small white villages and the occasional flocks of fishing boats. We sailed fast and silent, ignoring all hails. Captain William Hunter had one goal and one goal only.

San Angel.

Finally we were there. The passage was a bit tricky. A long, low island thick with trees protected the indifferent harbor from the sea.

"Doesn't look like much for all this fuss, does it, Uncle?" I asked as the two of us stood by the rail. Uncle Patch grunted in reply, but he, too, was scanning the little town before us.

San Angel was a small cluster of white buildings huddled around a tiny ivory-colored Catholic church. Behind it towered a tangled wall of dark green trees. The water in front was a deep blue. And not a sound or movement came from white or green or blue.

"I have no liking for this stillness," Uncle Patch muttered. "I have no liking for it at all."

Then the birds began swarming up in thousands, for an instant blotting out the little town in a fluttering wall of screaming white. Gulls, so many gulls, and my mind immediately cast back to the last time I had seen so many.

That was when they had risen like an evil white cloud over the horror that had been the derelict bark *Elizabeth Bingham.*

Their screaming cast a spell of silence over the decks of the *Aurora.* The closer we glided, the more apparent the destruction that was San Angel became. The harbor was empty and there was no giant bloodred pirate ship waiting for us with open gunports. In truth, there were no ships waiting at all. It was deserted, save for us. The little dock was cluttered with broken barrels and cases, fishing nets festooning the piers like seaweed. And the neat little houses gaped roofless at the cloudless sky.

And still the gulls rose.

"It's a fishing village," whispered Mr. Adams, coming up behind us. "Where are all the fishing boats?"

At that moment there was a sharp scraping sound from underneath us. Something was dragging against the *Aurora*'s cooper-sheathed bottom. Uncle Patch looked over the side and all the color drained from his ruddy face.

"Faith, Mr. Adams, they're all right here," he breathed in a dead voice. "You just have to know where to look."

I joined him at the railing and stared down into the azure water. I could just barely make it out, but I could see the faint outline of a fishing boat resting on the bottom of the harbor. It was the very tip of her single mast that was scraping against our hull. Other shadows loomed up out of the deeps.

"Sharks!" Mr. Alonzo cried from where he stood

clinging to the shrouds. "There's another! And another! Blessed Mary, the bay's alive with 'em!"

And by then even I could guess what the sharks were feeding on.

"Drop anchors, Mr. Adams," came Captain Hunter's unnaturally calm voice from where he stood high on the poop deck, "before we drive something through our hull. The bottom's too crowded around here for the *Aurora* to rest comfortably."

Our anchors splashing down into that polluted water was the loudest sound I had ever heard.

Once again I sat next to Uncle Patch and his medical kit, being rowed to another scene of death. The wind had shifted as soon as we had lowered the boats, and the reek that came boiling across the harbor to us from San Angel spoke volumes of burned buildings and ruin. Everything was quiet, as still as a tomb. Even Morgan's men, men who had seen slaughter and bodies piled atop bodies, sat silent and nervously fingered their cutlasses as the oars rose and fell. The gulls wheeled indignantly above us, and no one would look into the bright blue water, fearing the dark, soulless eyes of the sharks that might stare back.

Then we were standing on the little harbor street and that same water seemed pure as any angel's tears. "'S blood," Mr. Jeffers growled. "I was at Panama I was, in the thick o' it with Morgan himself. We did dark things that day, Lord forgive me. But this . . ." He just stood there, shaking his head.

The docks were thick with corruption and decay. Burros, cattle, and sheep had been slaughtered and left for the ravenous seagulls. We found no human bodies there or anywhere. That was almost worse than what we found aboard the *Elizabeth Bingham*. The crew had divided up into teams and began searching the town, desperately hoping to find someone, anyone, alive who could tell us what had caused this monstrous evil. As fast as they fanned out, they were back.

"Town's stripped bare, Cap'n," reported Mr. Alonzo, his suntanned face as pale as everyone else's. "Not a candle or a coil o' rope anywhere! Whoever did it looted and then burned everything, so they did!"

Captain Hunter nodded, not really listening. Like

the rest of us, he was staring at the front of the Catholic church that stood in San Angel's tiny town square. It had been a pretty little structure once, white and simple and holy. Now it stood desecrated, burned, and profaned. And all you had to do was glance at it to know who was responsible.

Across the entire front of that small, inoffensive building, someone had written a gigantic *H* in bright red paint.

"It's a trap," the captain said in that strange calm voice. "Baited in blood and betrayal. God's truth, what kind of brain has the man who can come up with this?"

I stood with my uncle, my heart in my mouth. Not a word had I spoken since we had landed, me who always has something to say. I was near thirteen and liked to think of myself as a man, with all the things I'd seen and done. Never had I felt more like a child since my mother had died. If seeing and hearing such things as this was what made a man, then it was a wonder anyone made it at all. I became aware of some kind of commotion behind us, but Captain Hunter was still speaking, and as far as I was concerned, his was the only voice in the world.

"This was one of his safe harbors. He came here for food and supplies and to unload treasure and loot. On those days when the *Red Queen* hove to in the harbor, it must have been like carnival time to these poor wretched devils. There must have been dancing in the streets."

Somewhere someone began to yell, "Cap'n! Cap'n!"

"William," Uncle Patch began, sounding concerned.

Captain Hunter's flat, empty voice didn't change a note. "They must have met her right at the dock, all of them singing and dancing. They had gathered flowers, flowers for the bloody *Red Queen*. Even their priest was there, come with his good book to bless their benefactor." Now the words were grinding out of him, like wheat crushed to flour between great millstones. "Their bodies went to feed the sharks."

My uncle put a hand on his arm. "For the love of mercy, William."

"Did any of them get nervous when she sailed past the fishing boats riding at anchor? Did they have time to scream before that floating horror opened her bloodstained sides and vomited death and destruction on them? They trusted him! See what he did to the people who trusted him!"

Now the commotion behind us was becoming too loud to ignore. I finally surfaced from the terrible reality around me long enough to recognize one of the voices. Mr. Tate was crowing his head off as he pounded his way through the packed pirates clustered around the captain.

"They be comin', sir! Can you not hear the drum? They be comin'!" he yelled, pushing men twice his size out of his way.

"Who's coming, Mr. Tate?" Captain Hunter said, never taking his eyes from the great dripping *H* on the side of the little church.

"The Spanish, Cap'n, that's who! The road east to Santiago is crawlin' with Spanish steel! Soldiers and cavalry, comin' at the double!"

"Aye, it's a trap!" snarled Uncle Patch. "A trap with jaws of steel closing on our necks!"

"There's a west road," the captain said, finally tearing his gaze from the church. "How fares it?"

"Another river of bloody Spaniard steel, Cap'n!" called Ezra Adain, one of the gunners' mates, running with his men from the opposite direction. "They must have started marching days ago to be here now! Someone sent word of what was goin' to happen. We've been betrayed!"

"Back to the *Aurora!*" Captain Hunter thundered, brandishing his cutlass back toward the harbor. "It's only a trap if we're foolish enough to stay in it! Run, you sea dogs, run!"

And run we did, pelting like madmen to the boats that rode on the polluted blue water. Fast we flew, oars stabbing into the very soul of the sea. Now we could all hear the drums, rumbling up from the converging roads. I imagined I even heard their boots, rising and falling, and my fevered mind swore I saw the sunlight flashing off silver breast-plates and helmets, with the gold-and-crimson banner of Spain over all.

"Row, curse ye, row!" Mr. Jeffers howled at his men. "The dons be indifferent sailors but the fiercest soldiers in the world! Remember Antwerp and row!"

Antwerp. My old tutor, Mr. Horne, had taught me the history of that sad city. Over one hundred years ago the soldiers of Philip II, he who had sent the Great Armada against England, had marched into the rebellious city of Antwerp. When they had marched out again, the city was destroyed and its people dead. Lord deliver us from the Spanish Fury.

Up the sides of the *Aurora* we scrambled, leaving our boats to tow behind. Our sails were up and just catching the wind when the first of the Spaniards burst out through the gutted white buildings of San Angel. Even across the water, I could hear their shouts of outrage and despair. I felt my face grow red with shame. They thought we were the villains who had slaughtered the innocents, like King Herod in the Bible. Their muskets roared out at us, but we were already out of range and beating out to sea.

We had cleared the long island that had failed to protect San Angel, and it looked as if we might be free. Then the second trap sprang.

"Sails, Cap'n!" came a loud cry from our truncated mainmast, and I spied a spindly arm pointing beyond our stern.

Captain Hunter turned and shaded his eyes with his hand. "Hardly seems fair, when you think about it."

Two heavily armed Spanish barks were standing in, racing toward the harbor passage on a quartering west wind. They flew huge red-and-gold banners and their sides were studded with too many guns.

"Saints!" my uncle snarled. "They should not be floating under the weight of so many bloody cannons, let alone closing on us!"

"The dons have always demanded good value for their gold, and they've always had a lot of gold," Captain Hunter replied. "Mr. Tate! Run up a Spanish flag and let's see if we can at least confuse our friends! Mr. Alonzo! On deck, sir, your services may soon be needed! Mr. Jeffers! Man your guns but keep the men below the bulkhead! Stand by, all! If you have any prayers, now would be a good time for them!"

I watched the men come pouring up on the deck in threes and fours and heard Mr. Jeffers whispering harshly to them as they arrived. "Steady, lads, steady! Crouch down! We're in for it now, we are!" Mr. Adams ran up our Spanish flag, but it looked a puny thing, not crackling and snapping with vengeance like the ones behind us. I didn't see how it could fool anyone. It didn't, of course, but it did buy us a few heartbeats of time, and that was what we most needed.

The flag and our disguise made the pursuing barks hesitate, but only for a moment. Then they were coming on again, closing on us rapidly. We would pay dearly for the missing sections of our masts and the sails they had held. The *Aurora* was simply not as fast as she had been before her alterations.

As we turned downwind, they were suddenly bracketing us, coming up one on each side, with ourselves trapped between them. And both of them but a few hundred yards off. Grim sailors stared at us. Not a word was spoken, not a curse hurled, just eyes that burned with cruel promises. They gave not a signal that I saw, but suddenly the bark on our left opened fire.

It was no warning shot, but a great roaring broadside. The cannonballs either fell short, skipped, or bounced ineffectively off our sides. The other Spanish ship, a little farther off, held her fire.

"The Spanish flag has failed, Mr. Adams!" Captain Hunter called out over the noise. "Run up the Union and see if that gets us anywhere!" As quickly as he spoke, the gaudy red-and-gold flag ran down and the solid old Union was hoisted up in its place. It made me feel good to see it fluttering where the Jolly Roger had flown so often. It did nothing for the dons, however. The two barks came angling in, ranging for better shots.

"So much for flags!" Captain Hunter shouted. "Mr. Jeffers, I suggest you run out your guns, and be quick!"

"Aye, aye, Cap'n! Stand to, lads! Get all that artwork off the sides! It's ball and powder now and the devil take the hindmost!"

With a deadly speed, men were ripping away the painted canvas gunports from the sides of the *Aurora,* exposing the real ones underneath. The second our gunports sprang open, both barks opened fire on us! They were now so close that they could not miss, and their shot pounded against the hull. The valiant *Aurora* shuddered as ball after ball struck home.

"Why are we not returning fire?" I demanded of Uncle Patch. He stood there grim as death. There was nothing my uncle hated more than battle. He considered it a waste, and I had often wondered, if that was his opinion, why he had ever gone to sea for the navy.

"Mr. Jeffers is getting a feel for them, Davy. It takes a cold, steady man to calculate cannons. If you do it right, it costs you. If you do it wrong, it costs you even more!"

I watched Mr. Jeffers and realized that he was counting. I could see his lips move and his head nod. The Spanish barks fired again, the port one first, the starboard one mere seconds later. The first was firing solid shot, the second chain, meant to cut through our lines and men. Neither had any effect on Mr. Jeffers.

"Brave they are, but slow, lads! Roll 'em out and we'll touch 'em up good! Starboard fire!"

Our starboard guns roared out and the crews immediately began to reload. As they feverishly worked, Mr. Jeffers literally skipped across the deck to where the other crews awaited his orders.

"Larboard fire!"

Now the port guns blazed away, and for the briefest moment their Spanish target disappeared in billowing white clouds, only to reappear as their own guns fired. Barely a minute and a half passed before Mr. Jeffers was back with his original guns.

"Starboard fire!"

From where Uncle Patch had stuffed me, I watched the starboard guns hammer their target. Then I turned, my eyes following the sprinting Mr. Jeffers.

"Larboard fire!"

This time our guns came home on the heavy Spanish ship. Our broadside blew gaping holes into the rails of the bark, and I saw at least two of their great guns upset and crashing back across their decks. More broadsides rang out. The dons were brave but slow, between them managing to get off but one broadside to our two. Cannons roared again, and I clapped my hands over my ears and thanked our stars that neither of our enemies was the *Concepcion,* nor had any of their crews trained under her captain, Don Esteban de Reyes. He would have handed us our heads by now, even with two barks instead of his great war galleon. Just then, part of our starboard railing exploded into splinters, and I feared for our mainmast and the men crouched beneath it.

Then we hulled the starboard bark, and her

foremast came crashing down. She peeled away from us, her crew striving to clear her forecastle and keep her afloat. We pulled away from her but her sister kept coming, still firing away at us, cheered on by the sailors of the crippled bark.

But even stripped of her topgallant masts, the *Aurora* was the superior ship, and with the wind full behind us the remaining bark didn't stand a chance of catching us. Still, far into the night she pursued us, blazing away with her bow-chasers until she finally dropped below the horizon and out of range.

CHAPTER 6

Butcher's Bill

FROM ALL I could tell, the *Aurora* was sound in body, though the Spanish broadsides had shattered her limbs. The main topmast was gone at the partners, shot clean away, and the foremast had been so badly sprung, a strong wind would snap it in two like a dry stick. The whipstaff had been shot through, and the crew had rigged a makeshift, meanwhile steering the frigate by means of pulling on ropes belowdecks, directed by a crewman shouting orders down through the cockpit.

But most of this I learned later, for busy were my uncle and I with the wounded. Three men had been killed outright: George Sawyer, Lloyd Jones, and Pondoo, who was one of the score or so of freed slaves who had willingly joined our crew. I had come to know these three men over our months at sea, and their deaths hit me hard. George Sawyer had been a navy man, mostly silent, but friendly and always willing to give a crewmate a rest by taking on part of his job. Jones had been a Welshman who loved a joke and a song, aimed his cannon as true as any could wish, and was our best fiddler. Pondoo, if that were even his real name, we had taken from our first prize. The poor man had been a slave, belonging to the Spanish captain of the very first privateer we had taken. When he heard our crew's voices, he had pleaded, "I know English! Take me from this man, please. He beats me."

Strong as any ox, many a time he had talked to me in his soft voice of his harsh life. He was taken from Africa, he had said, when he was but a child, and for a time was a slave on Tortuga, when that island was in English hands. Taken then by the French and sold to the Spanish captain, he lived a life of misery for many years. Once I had asked if he wished to go back to Africa.

"Don't know," he had said quietly. "My whole family was taken. What is Africa without my family?" His hope was that somehow he could find his mother, father, brothers, and sister in the New World, but that was a dim enough wish. Come to that, he thought his family might have died on the slave ship coming over from Africa, for on it they were treated like animals, separated one from the other, and chained, and half or more of them had died.

But though we had lost those three, the seventeen others who were wounded still had hopes of living, and my uncle worked like a dog over them, stitching and splinting, patching them up as best he could. It was remarkable to me always that the men seldom cried out or complained, even with the most terrible wounds. One old fellow, Davis by name, was placed on the operating table by some of his shipmates. The moment my uncle cut away Davis's shirt, he shook his head. A horrible long spear of wood, probably part of a spar, had pierced him through the chest.

Blood dripped from the corners of his mouth. He said in a wheeze, "It's bad, ain't it, Doctor?"

"Bad enough," Uncle Patch said shortly. "Your lung is pierced, Davis."

He nodded, his eyes dull. "Be I goin'?" he asked in that same rusty wheeze.

"I'll do what I can," said my uncle.

Old Davis raised a hand, flailed it, and caught my uncle's wrist. "Be I dyin'?" he said with a grim insistence.

My uncle gently released the clutching hand. "Davis, I think you are."

"Put me aside, then," Davis answered at once. "Work on them as can be saved."

"One thing at a time," insisted my uncle.

But Davis died before Uncle Patch could even remove the splinter, and a moment later we were dealing with a man who had a fractured skull and concussion of the brain.

Hours passed in this bloody work. Even with five lanterns hung, the light was bad, and my uncle's eyes soon grew nearly as red as cherries from the strain. We lost no more patients, though, and in the small hours before dawn we were down to broken arms and ugly bruises that were spectacular but not dangerous.

We were dealing with the worst of these, a sailor named York with a broken arm, when I became aware of someone behind me. I looked over my shoulder and saw that Captain Hunter had come below. His face was pale as he stared at my uncle, who was well-nigh drenched with blood.

"Davy," Uncle Patch said sternly, "strap him down."

"You ain't goin' to cut, are ye?" asked York, clearly terrified that he was going to lose his arm.

"No, lad," my uncle assured him. "This is going to hurt like the very devil, though, and 'tis better if you can't thrash about."

I fastened the buckles of the big leather straps and put a length of leather between York's teeth. "Bite on that when it hurts."

"Ready?" asked Uncle Patch. He wrenched the broken arm back into shape. York's whole body arched, and he bit down hard on the leather. A high-pitched *eeeee,* almost more a whistle than a cry, escaped from him, his eyes rolled up in his head, and he passed out.

"He's fainted," I said.

"That's a mercy, anyway," shot back Uncle Patch, feeling the arm to make sure the bones were in position to knit together. Then, working with a speed that few surgeons could equal, he splinted the arm and bound the splints tight with bandages. He raised his head and glared at Captain Hunter. "Four men dead already," he said in an accusing voice. "William, what d'ye think you're about? Steele's a butcher! When are you going to put an end to his capers?"

Roughly Captain Hunter snarled, "As soon as ever may be."

"It should have been long before now," grumbled Uncle Patch. "Before he slaughtered that town. Before he led us into his bloody trap!"

I felt my cheeks grow hot. What bothered me was something I had been thinking ever since I had first heard the word "trap" back in San Angel. Had the drunken sailor been a spy, too? Was his babbling meant to lure us to destruction? If so . . . if so, then I was to blame for the deaths of those men, for I had given the word to Captain Hunter to sail to San Angel.

"I don't need a lecture, Doctor," the captain said in such a cold voice that I looked at him in surprise. His eyes were level and unblinking. There was something of a serpent's stare in those eyes.

"Ye need something!" my uncle growled as he tied off the last bandage.

"Not from you!" Captain Hunter's words were like the lash of a whip. "I tell you, Doctor, that I shall kill Jack Steele. If I have so much as a plank to sit on, a rag to hoist as sail, and one cannon to fire, I will kill that man or die myself."

"William—," began Uncle Patch.

"Give me the report!" Hunter snapped. "What is the butcher's bill?"

With his own weary face set in hard lines of anger, my uncle said through clenched teeth, "Sixteen wounded, three in danger of death. Four dead—Davis, Pondoo, Jones, and Sawyer. The rest I will answer for, if their wounds do not mortify."

"I will enter that into the log." The captain turned on his heel and stalked away.

We had only one more patient, a man with a broken finger, and that was set easily enough. Then we made the rounds and checked on the men we had treated. Uncle Patch had given them all rum with the alcoholic tincture of opium added, and all were asleep, or rather, unconscious. "I believe we may turn in for this night of Our Lord," murmured Uncle Patch.

We washed ourselves as well as we could in basins, though my uncle had to scrub hard with a pumice stone to remove the caked blood from his forearms and fingers. At last we crept into the small booth of the sleeping cabin that we shared. He rolled into his cot, and I climbed into my hammock. "Prayers," Uncle Patch said, and I whispered my evening devotions.

He blew out the single lantern, plunging us into darkness. After a few moments, I asked, "Did I cause all this misery, then, by being fooled by the drunk in the King's Mercy?"

"No, lad," came my uncle's kind voice. "Who knows if the drunkard's tale was true or false? Not I, nor the captain. Jack Steele is cracked in the brain, I think. Perhaps someone in San Angel looked at him the wrong way, or smiled when he should not have. Or, yes, it could have all been a deep-laid trap to murder us and take William off his trail. 'Tis no shame if that's the case, for older heads than yours were misled."

"I've never seen the captain that angry."

I heard a long, drawn-out sigh in the darkness. "Faith, Davy, I worry about my friend. His mother and father were both killed by Steele when William was hardly older than you are now. And just when William thinks he has the rogue in his hands, Steele slips through his fingers. Now all this death weighs heavily upon him. Sawyer was what they call William's sea-daddy when William was just a midshipman. It was Sawyer who showed him the ropes and taught him to tie his square knots, bowlines, and sheepshanks. It's as if . . ."

His voice trailed off, and for long moments I thought that he had gone to sleep in midsentence, but then he spoke again. "As if William has been broken in some way. He's a smart man, the smartest man I've known, but he's aware of that intelligence within himself. When Steele out-thinks him, beats him at his own game, William blames himself. In some way his mind has been cracked by all this, and I fear the pieces no longer fit."

I suppose I must have slept in the few hours that remained of that night, but I cannot remember for sure. Indeed, all the next few weeks are a blur of action in my memory. The next morning Captain

Hunter read the funeral service over the bodies of our shipmates, as he had done so many times before, and we dropped them into the ocean. Their bodies had been sewn into hammocks and weighted with round shot at their feet, and the four vanished into the depths of the water.

Perhaps that day, perhaps the next, Captain Hunter ordered the men to throw off the *Aurora*'s disguise. Up went our topgallant masts again, and out came the black and yellow paint to restore her to her former looks. Our figurehead came out of the hold and returned to her place below the bowsprit.

We took two ships in close succession, a French privateer first and then a Spanish one. Neither stood a chance. Our crew stripped them of powder, shot, and cargo, and Captain Hunter interrogated their captains in his cabin. From the deck we could hear his voice raised, almost raving, as he demanded to know any news of Jack Steele.

A day later we overhauled a sloop flying the Jolly Roger. She seemed to strike her colors, but then as we drew alongside, she opened up with a broadside. Furious, Captain Hunter gave the order to fire into her, and our gunners pounded the little craft so hard that she keeled over almost at once. I saw bodies floating on the surface, but by the time we had closed the few hundred yards that separated us, the sloop had sunk.

"Search for survivors, sir?" asked Mr. Warburton.

"No," Captain Hunter snapped. "Let 'em learn not to offer resistance if they hope to live."

I could not help thinking that Jack Steele must be very much like this. Somehow, Captain Hunter was becoming the very thing he hated most, losing his humanity in his desire to strike vengeance at Steele. The captain never laughed anymore, where once he was fast to roar out with the sheer joy of play-acting the part of pirate. Now his face was always cold, and his voice showed no touch of mercy.

The captains of the ships we took always rowed back to their stripped vessels with speed born of fear. Indeed, more than once I thought that only Uncle Patch's presence aboard the *Aurora* kept Captain Hunter from torturing his captives to see if they knew anything of Steele.

The captain's anger came to a head some days later. The lookout had reported a sail hull-down and to windward of us. Captain Hunter altered course so that our paths gradually converged over six hours of sailing, and by that time we could see the other vessel plain: a bark flying the flag of an English merchant ship.

"Veer off, Cap'n?" asked Mr. Warburton at the whipstaff.

"Belay that!" shouted Captain Hunter. "We'll take her."

"English, Cap'n?" asked Mr. Warburton uneasily.

Uncle Patch was standing at the leeward rail. He came over with concern in his expression. "William, you cannot—," he began.

Captain Hunter whirled on him, his face flaming. "Cannot? Cannot, sir?" He looked forward and called, "Mr. Adams! To my cabin now!" And in a furious whisper, he said to my uncle, "You too, sir. We have a question to settle at once."

I followed. As soon as Mr. Adams had closed the door, Captain Hunter said to him, "Mr. Adams, as first mate of this vessel, kindly tell the doctor here who is the captain aboard this ship!"

Mr. Adams blinked in surprise and unease. "Sir?"

"Fire and brimstone, man! Who is the captain?" roared Captain Hunter.

"Y-you are, sir," said Mr. Adams.

"Very good. You may go."

And when Mr. Adams had left us, Captain Hunter said to my uncle, "You are never—*never*—to stand upon my quarterdeck and tell me what I can or cannot do, Doctor. If you do so even once more, I shall have you clapped in irons. Is that plain?"

"Aye, sir," said my uncle stiffly.

We did not try to take the English vessel, for she suddenly seemed aware of us. She had the wind gage—that is, the wind was blowing from her direction toward us—and so her captain could decide whether to let us approach or not. Something about the *Aurora* must have stirred his suspicion, for suddenly the bark made all sail and stood away from us. She was smaller, lighter, and faster, and by sunset it was clear she would outrun us. We gave up the chase in the gathering twilight.

From that day the mood aboard the ship changed. A ship is like a little village, with people so used to one another's ways and words that nothing goes unnoticed or unremarked. I felt a kind of tension in the air, and it did not take long to realize that it was between the old buccaneers who had belonged to Sir Henry Morgan's crews and the smaller number who were navy men. The latter were appalled at Captain Hunter's intention to attack a British ship. The former seemed happy with the change. "More to chink in our pockets, mates," one of them said with a chuckle.

But a third party of Morgan's men was deeply upset. "If this 'ere captain goes off 'is 'ead an' sinks English ships," one of them complained, "why, ye can kiss our pardons good-bye, and ye may lay to that!" He rubbed his neck. "I don't fancy doin' a hangman's jig at the end of a rope, not I."

I hated to bother my uncle with my fears and worries, but it seemed to me that Captain Hunter was within an ace of turning pirate for real. And then what would become of us all?

For many days we had been making our way north and east, heading, I guessed, to the little low island called Cruzado in the southern Bahamas, between Inagua Island and the Caicos and Turks Islands. A band of pirates had made a small settlement there, and we needed to replace our damaged foremast before a storm could rise and break it in two.

Captain Hunter nursed the ship along. His navigation was usually good, but this time his reckoning was off. We were too far south and east, and we came within sight of a ragged scattering of small islands, hardly more than rocks. Toward sunset, Mr. Adams climbed to the maintop to scan them with his telescope, and when he returned to the deck, he said, "I think the island in the far distance is Salt Cay, sir. We must be south of Grand Turk."

Captain Hunter cursed at that. "Then we have to come about. Our course must be northwest by north, and—".

"A ship!" cried the sailor on lookout duty.

"Where away?" the captain called back.

"Fine on the larboard bow," the lookout answered.

I could see nothing from the deck. Captain Hunter scrambled up the shrouds, though, and stared off to the east. "It's the *Fury*," he called down at last, and I breathed a little easier. The *Fury* was a sloop under the command of John Barrel, a right, true buccaneer and a friend of ours from back in the early part of the year.

Captain Hunter slid down a backstay like a boy, dropped to the deck, and ordered, "Clear for action."

I could not believe my ears. The one-legged John Barrel had been loyal to us when we were under heavy fire in Tortuga Harbor. It would be monstrous to repay his loyalty with cannon fire.

But then I realized that Barrel knew Steele—had even sailed with him—and that he was just the sort of connection to Steele that the captain wanted. I ran below to my uncle, who was reading by the glow of a lantern, and gasped out the news.

"The devil!" he exclaimed, clapping his book shut. "Let me have a word with William."

We hurried back to the deck. The men had run out the larboard cannons, though they looked uneasy and unsure of themselves.

"Let him come within pistol-shot range," Captain Hunter ordered. "Then we shall take him."

I looked over the rail. The *Fury* had closed fast, coming down with the wind. She was only two hundred yards away.

And then, with surprising speed, she shifted her sails, spun about to show us her broadside, and opened fire!

CHAPTER 7

Jury Attacks

GRAPESHOT RIPPED ACROSS our decks, shredding men and lines and sails. Railing flew into splinters and one of our guns was thrown over, crushing half of its crew under two tons of iron. Men screamed and cursed, and a dazed Captain Hunter stood there, his cutlass limp in his hand. Uncle Patch yanked him around and shouted into his blank face.

"Awake, William!" he roared. "The devil's dealt new cards and you haven't even picked up your hand!"

Fire came billowing back into the captain's eyes, and for a horrible moment I thought he was going to strike my uncle, and that would mean the end of us. Then something shiny and sharp came sailing over the larboard railing and bit into the black wood with a meaty thud. Both Uncle Patch and Captain Hunter stared at it.

"Boarders!" Uncle Patch snarled with a curse.

More of the silver hooks were flying up and over now just as the *Fury* emptied another broadside into our starboard. I ran to the side to see what was going on, only to be yanked back by my uncle after a glimpse.

"Have ye gone brainless as well?" he thundered. "Down, ye young fool, down!"

I was shoved down onto the deck, but I had seen what I had seen. Three longboats loaded to the gunnels with pirates were lashing themselves to our port side. While we had been concentrating on the *Fury*, they had crept up on us, silent as fever. And now they were roaring up our sides, all screams and steel.

And every one of them had a strip of red silk tied to his right arm. It was a uniform of sorts, the red mark of men who sailed for Jack Steele.

"No quarter, ye dogs!" a deep voice boomed from the deck of the *Fury*. "None asked, none given!"

Now the grappling hooks came flying from the decks of the *Fury* as her crew fought to lash her tight to the *Aurora*. Men were leaping over and landing on our decks, cutlasses flashing in the fading light. And every one wore a strip of bright crimson silk.

"They've hurt my ship," said Captain Hunter in a voice lost in wonder. Then his eyes flashed with that old Hunter fire. "To me, *Aurora*! Repel boarders!" And he was rushing down to where his crew was just beginning to rally against the invaders.

"Aye, just rush in and get your simple English brains knocked out!" Uncle Patch yelled over the clash of battle. "'Tis so much better knowing we have a plan! Mr. Warburton!"

"Aye, Doctor?" rumbled our giant helmsman.

"Watch my fool of a nephew! 'Tis his help I'll be needing before all this is down and done! I've got to help Hunter!" He turned back to me and slapped a gully, a sailor's knife, into my hand. "Eyes, legs, liver, and lights—forget about honorable fighting! Any dog that attacks a boy doesn't deserve it! Stab fast, get away, and run like the devil!"

With these words, Uncle Patch drew his own

sword and was about to leap down after the captain when he was stopped by a peal of cruel laughter from the decks of the *Fury*. He stared into the billowing cannon smoke and snapped a string of curses that made even Mr. Warburton step back.

"'S blood! Not him!" Then he was down the stairs into the battle. I stared over to where that stout sloop rode, grappled tight against us. A man I momentarily mistook for John Barrel stood there, stripped to the waist and roaring with laughter. His head and body and arms were covered with blue tattoos that swirled and twisted over him like flat snakes writhing under his skin. And I knew why my uncle had sworn so. If I had had his talent for cursing, I would have done so myself.

The man roared, "At them, ye bloodless swine! No quarter, says I! No quarter and the devil take the hindmost!"

The last time I had seen him, Jessie and I had been running from a plantation house on the island of Tortuga and from a smiling, pale man we had known as Mr. Robert Meade. Robert Meade had turned out to be Jack Steele, and this grinning monster was one of his major lieutenants, the infamous pirate, Shark. I had thought him dead, for Captain Hunter had fired a pistol at him from close range, but the wound must not have been mortal.

Even as I stared, the pirate captain grabbed a loose line, wrapped it around his arm, and swung flying across to the deck of the *Aurora*. His cutlass gleamed as he fell roaring into the mass of struggling, straining men.

I wish I could give a clear account of the battle that raged that day, but in truth all that comes to me now as I write is a series of pictures, flashes of the fight. I will try to be faithful to them.

The pirates had the element of surprise, but I'm sure they had no idea of who made up the bulk of our crew. Morgan's old buccaneers shook off their shock in short order and came back at the invaders, nasty grins on their seamed brown faces. This wasn't playacting, this was butcher's work, and that was work they understood full well. I had a lord's view of it all, there on the quarterdeck with Mr. Warburton towering over me, a monstrous sword in his massive hand. I know not where he found it. He might have taken it from a dead Viking, for all I knew. I clutched my gully in a death grip and prepared to sell my life dearly.

The *Fury* could no longer fire her broadsides at us, for she was too close and would have done as much damage to herself as to the *Aurora*. So it was hand to hand and man to man, and the blood flowed across our littered deck.

I saw Mr. Adams, as gentle a man as ever wore the king's uniform, screaming like a madman as he discharged a pistol into the face of a man who was about to split his skull with the edge of a cutlass.

I saw Mr. Adain, he who had warned us about the Spanish advance at San Angel, go down with a fierce cut across his belly. He died in a gush of blood, clasping his innards.

I had never seen a boarding raid before. In the past the *Aurora* had always fired only one round at her victims, forcing them to strike their flags. Every time we had boarded without a fight.

This was different. This was men hacking away at one another like butchers slicing up a side of beef. There was none of the elegant parry and thrust I had witnessed when Captain Hunter and Uncle Patch had practiced at singlestick in the little yard behind the King's Mercy.

The blades swung savagely back and forth, like sickles harvesting wheat. Where the edges struck, limbs flew and blood spurted in fountains. Where the sides struck, skulls split and arms snapped. The noise, the howling and growling and screaming, battered against my ears. The only mercy was that the musket fire had stopped, for the sharpshooters had no time to reload.

Mr. Warburton stood at the edge of the quarter-deck, swinging his giant sword back and forth. Pirates were trying to come up the stairs and take control of the whipstaff. But to do that they'd have to get past the towering helmsman, and that wasn't likely to happen.

"Not my station!" Mr. Warburton roared, smashing another pirate on the top of the head so that he fell like a sack of wet flour. "Nobody barges onto my station!"

Then I heard it again. That silver meaty *thunk* that meant another grappling hook had gone home. I looked over to where it had landed. It dug into the splitting railing wood, gouging in as it was dragged tight. A cry of triumph came up from below. Mr. Warburton was busy tossing another pirate off the deck, so I gathered all my courage, crept over to the railing, and looked over the side. Sure enough, three pirates were swarming up the side, daggers tight in their teeth. They grinned around the steel at me. I tried to pull the hook free, but it was in too deep and the weight of the pirates kept pulling it ever deeper. Then I could have sworn I heard a voice snap, "Is that the only idea you can come up with, you great mooncalf?" And suddenly it wasn't.

I yanked out the gully Uncle Patch had thrust upon me, and I hacked at the rope. The blade was marvelously sharp and sliced through the hemp braids like a razor. The first pirate was almost upon me, his hand reaching out, his eyes wide as he realized what I was doing. The rope parted, and he and his two companions fell tumbling back into the water. I felt right proud of myself.

Then Mr. Warburton fell on me.

All the breath went out of me in a whoosh and I thought that I had been crushed to death. It took me precious moments to recover myself and push the valiant helmsman off me. He rolled over onto his back, and I saw the great oozing bruise on the side of his head that had brought him down. Something had clipped him right fair. Quickly I checked his eyes and pulse as Uncle Patch had taught me. He was alive but not going anywhere. Grasping my gully, I rushed to what was left of the railing and looked down onto the deck below.

The battle still raged, but I saw a weariness about it now. The fighters had spent their initial fury and now bashed at one another with a mechanical viciousness that was even more frightening than their previous rage. And then I noticed who was battling away at the foot of the ladder, and I almost cried out in horror.

Uncle Patch and Shark stood toe-to-toe and slashed away at each other with their cutlasses. There was no retreating back and forth. They stood their ground, neither giving an inch as they hacked and blocked, each straining to get past the other's guard. My uncle had thrown off his coat. His shirt, never the cleanest, was now stiff with blood and sweat. His copper-red hair had come loose from its ribbon and flew all over his head like a lion's mane. And even from where I was high above him, I could hear him swearing under his breath. At least I assumed he was swearing. During the battle he had switched from English to Gaelic.

Shark was also sweating, the heavy beads sheeting off his body and dripping off his shaved head. He was so slick with it, his spiraling blue tattoos seemed to actually twist and squirm around on his arms and chest. Unlike Uncle Patch, Shark didn't say a word. He just swung away at his opponent and grinned.

It was a cold, white grin with too many pointed teeth.

Slowly—and still muttering away in the language of his father's fathers—Uncle Patch began to force Shark back toward the cabin door beneath me. Soon the pirate would be right up against the wood. Then suddenly Shark began to laugh. It was a wild, ugly laugh that cut through all the battle noise like a barracuda through a school of fat fish. A second later I saw what Shark saw: a pirate with a spent musket rearing up behind Uncle Patch. With a roundhouse swing, he brought the useless weapon around and smashed my uncle on the side of his head. Uncle Patch went down like a poleaxed steer. Now I did cry out, for the pirate again raised the shattered musket like a club and prepared to open Uncle Patch's skull like a ripe melon.

And there was nothing I could do about it!

Then a pistol roared, and the pirate arched his back as his chest sent out a gush of blood. The force of the blast threw him stumbling across my uncle and into Shark. The pirate chief roared in rage as the body of his own man slammed him back into the wall. They were barely down before the dead body was hurled to one side and Shark was staggering back to his feet.

"Careful, boy," he snarled. "Ye keep that up and someone's liable t' get hurt."

Captain Hunter tossed aside the pistol with which he had saved my uncle's life, and drew his cutlass. "Oh, I can almost guarantee someone is. It is Shark, is it not?"

"Last time I clapped eyes on ye," rumbled Shark, "ye creased my skull with a pistol ball."

"Too bad my aim was off."

"That mouth is gonna get you killed, boyo—right now!" And Shark launched himself over the living and the dead, his heavy cutlass already swinging down for a killing blow.

Captain Hunter got his own blade up just in time to parry Shark's thrust, and then they were at each other. Their cutlasses rang like broken bells every time they struck. This was no head-to-head like Shark and Uncle Patch. They were back and forth across the deck, leaping and thrusting and cutting. Never a word they said to each other as they went at it like wolves over a dead deer.

Slowly the fighting around them began to stop as both sides became aware of the great battle going on. Now the two men were in the middle of a great circle on the *Aurora*'s main deck. It was almost like some battle of old Irish warriors out of the stories my mother used to tell me, as much dance and stamina as swordplay and skill. Captain Hunter smiled grimly as he worked, but Shark grinned, teeth visible from ear to ear.

Finally the tip of the captain's cutlass sliced through the skin and muscle on Shark's chest. Blood began to pour forth, gushing over his tattoos, almost obscuring them. He laughed and leaped forward, spraying blood and sweat everywhere, and drove the point of his blade into Captain Hunter's left shoulder. The captain fell back from the pain, and in that instant Shark, with a great wide sweep of his blade, sent the captain's cutlass flying from his hand.

"You're mine, boyo!" Shark laughed as he drew back for the killing stroke. Captain Hunter dropped to one knee, his injured left arm hanging limp. But his right arm swung down and came back with a dagger he had in his boot. The swing continued under the gleaming cutlass and slammed in below Shark's tattooed breastbone. The pirate looked down at the hilt in the center of his chest and then at Captain Hunter, who was painfully climbing to his feet.

"My aim is better now, Shark."

Then Shark began to grin again and the red blood gushed from between his clenched teeth. "Your ship's wrecked. Crew's wrecked. Name's wrecked. Compliments o' Cap'n Steele, laddie, compliments o' . . ." His eyes rolled up into his head and he pitched forward, stark dead, onto the deck.

For a moment, the only thing I could hear was Captain Hunter's labored breathing. Then he did the most amazing thing. He reached down, grabbed the dead pirate by his belt and shoulder, and with a grunt of effort heaved the body up over his head.

"Shark is dead! Shark is dead!" he shouted, and threw the compact body over the side of the *Aurora*. I heard it crash into one of the longboats.

Nothing happened for another second, but then a wailing cry came up from the pirate invaders. "Shark is dead!" And suddenly they were breaking for the remaining longboats, all the fight gone out of them. It was a total rout. Our men harried them every step of the way, and many of our foes died before the longboats began to pull away.

Mr. Jeffers and his crew rolled out one of the guns and commenced firing as fast as they could. I saw another of the longboats shatter, hurling its desperate crew into the air and into the sea.

As for me, I flew down the ladder two steps at a time until I finally reached my uncle. He lay in an untidy heap on the deck, deadly pale, but to my joy he was still breathing. Blood flowed from a huge lump above his left temple. I tore the sleeve off his grimy shirt—it was ruined anyway—and began to use it to dress his wound.

"Have a care," mumbled a groggy voice. "That was my favorite white shirt."

"Forget the shirt." I worked feverishly trying to stop the blood from flowing.

"Ye have the delicate touch of a blacksmith, ye daft lad! Who told ye that ye were any kind o' surgeon?"

"'Twas yourself, ye fool!" I shouted at him, tears streaming down my face. "Now, shut up and let me save your useless life!"

"There's others worse hurt," he whispered, and then mercifully for both of us, he passed out.

When I had finished, I looked around from where I knelt over my unconscious uncle on the deck. All around lay the dead and wounded.

Nearby Captain Hunter stood looking dazed. "Mr. Adams."

"Aye, sir?"

"Get some men with axes and cut the *Fury* loose. Then we can tend to our own."

"Should we search her first, Cap'n?" Mr. Adams was swaying back and forth but his voice was steady.

"I doubt there's anyone alive left aboard, but—"

Then a loud crash burst from the captured sloop. A furious pounding came from somewhere aboard her. Quick as a flash, a crewman leaped over the side and onto the *Fury.* With a few well-timed swings of an ax, he burst open the door to the cabin.

And out of the doorway lumbered the enraged figure of John Barrel, his wooden leg thumping loudly on the deck. "My sloop! What have the bloody dogs done to me poor, poor sloop?"

CHAPTER 8

Bloody Work

OUR CREWMEN knocked open the hatches on the *Fury*'s deck, and through them men rushed, blinking and staring about fiercely. One of them pointed to Barrel and yelled, "What's a-do, John? Be we prisoners o' these men or partners?"

"Belay your gab, Baulk," Captain Barrel shot back. "D'ye see chains on your ankles?" He shot a glance at the *Aurora*. "Cap'n Hunter's took back the *Fury* for us from Shark's men!"

I was trying to count. Eight, nine . . . was that all? With Captain Barrel, that meant only ten men of the *Fury*'s crew of forty or so were accounted for. But I had no time to reflect on that. Uncle

Patch was calling for me. He had staggered to his feet, pulling himself up by a dangling line, and he was thundering, "Davy! Confound you, we must get to the sick berth! We'll have our hands full soon enough!"

I ran to him and he threw an arm over my shoulder. I have said that my uncle was tall and broad-shouldered. He was also most awkwardly heavy, and now he smelled strongly of gunpowder and sweat. We all but tumbled down to the sick berth, where he stood steadying himself with a hand against a bulkhead. He ripped my improvised bandage off. "Take a quick look at this," he growled, bending his head and holding his long red hair clenched in one hand. "Do I need stitches?"

I lifted a lantern. An ugly lump was swelling just behind his temple, and it had a split in it and was still oozing blood. But by now I knew wounds well enough. "Stitches later, but for now a compress will do," I said. "Sit and I'll prepare one."

"The devil you will," he said shortly. "There's no time, for I hear them coming already with that heavy tread of those bearing the hurt. I rely on you, Davy."

Our first patient was white from the loss of blood, and a jet of it spurted from a wound on his upper left arm with every pulse of his heart. "Artery," my uncle said. "Pressure on it, Davy!"

A year earlier, I would have been too squeamish to plunge my finger into the wound, find the artery, and compress it, but habit had made that nothing to me. Beneath my finger I could feel the steady throbbing. Uncle Patch fetched a needle already threaded with fine catgut. "So," he said. "Higher. Yes, I see. A clean cut, saints be praised. Hold him still!"

With darting movements almost quicker than I could follow, Uncle Patch sewed the two ends of the artery together, made sure the mended place was not leaking, and then sewed up the wound, swaying slightly. Already two or three more wounded were waiting for us. "See which needs to be next," ordered my uncle, tottering on his feet.

The wounded were backing up. "Is Mr. Grice unhurt?" Uncle Patch asked one of the sailors.

"Aye, sir, sound an' whole," the man answered.

"Then get him down here at once. Davy, can you stitch this man up?"

That was something I had never done before. My uncle handed me a curved needle and in a few words told me how to take the stitches. "He has passed out, so he should give you no trouble," he said. "Now put that man up here."

We had only the one operating table, but it was broad enough for two to lie abreast, or rather head to foot, for that was the way the second man was placed there. He had an ugly fracture of the ribs, with bone piercing through the flesh.

I had time just for a glance as I passed the needle through living flesh, drawing together the lips of the wound as I had seen my uncle do. I fear my stitches were not as neat as his, or as fast, but at last I had put seventeen in and pulled the wound together. "Done!" I said.

"Good enough." My uncle turned to the sailors. "Get this man into a hammock and let's have the one with the bloodied head next. Lively!"

Before long, Uncle Patch had to kneel on the deck, so dizzy was he with his own hurt, but old Phineas Grice, the sailmaker, could stitch as well as he and had sewn up his shipmates before this. He and I shared the table. The hardest patients were those who were least hurt, for they were conscious of the pain. Mr. Grice took these.

Even with the three of us working, it took hours. At last my uncle was tending to the last patient, Mr. Vickery, a stoic old gray-haired buccaneer, setting his broken leg and plucking some painful but not lethal splinters from his thigh. "All done?" Uncle Patch asked in a dazed voice. "All the conscious men have had their rum?"

No, they had not, for I had been kept too busy working on them. But I ran to fetch it and used the better part of a bottle pouring the tots for our survivors. The injured had spilled out of the sick berth. Their hammocks hung as far forward as the foot of the foremast. I almost wondered if we had enough sailors left on two feet to sail the *Aurora*.

With a hand clapped to his head, Uncle Patch spoke to every conscious man, offering encouragement, a kind word, an awkward joke or two. Then he and I went back to the compartment we shared, and he sank groaning into a chair. "Bandage this for me now," he said, pointing to the wound behind his head.

I wound the bandage around, padding the great

lump that now showed all the way through his coppery red hair. "Done," I told him.

He looked up at me. "Look into my eyes," he said. "Are my pupils of equal size?"

I stared hard into his green eyes, undecided for a time whether the left was the smallest bit larger than the right. But that was a trick of the lantern light. "They are," I said at last.

"Bring the lantern close and see if they get smaller at the same rate." I shone the light into his face, and he winced. "Saint Joseph, but that sends lances into my brain!"

"They look the same," I said, shading the lantern.

"Good. Then I have no bleeding in the brain, let us hope. Davy, be a good lad and fetch me a small glass of brandy, for I'm shaking like a man with the palsy."

I brought it, and he tossed it off in three gulps. Then he held out his hand. "Help me up, now, and onto the deck. Let us see what's what up there."

He had to lean on me even more heavily going up than he had coming down, but we emerged at last. The crew had cleaned up the deck, to a point. "Mr. Adams," my uncle croaked feebly. "What of the day?"

"Are you all right, sir?" Mr. Adams asked, his beefy English face showing his shock.

Uncle Patch waved his concern away. "I shall do. How many dead?"

Mr. Adams looked around. "Twenty-seven of the enemy that I counted. Barrel's men heaved all the pirates over the rail without so much as a by-your-leave."

"We killed twenty-seven of them?" I asked, startled.

Mr. Adams lowered his voice. "'Twas twenty-seven they heaved overboard. I have my suspicions that not all were dead."

I was staring at a long row of white forms, like mummies stretched out on the deck. These were our men—ten, eleven, a round dozen of them, dead and sewn up into their hammocks.

"Where's the captain?" Uncle Patch asked. "He was wounded, I know, but he did not report to sick berth. How is it with him?"

"He had me tie up his cuts," Mr. Adams told him. "He said he would have you do a proper job in time."

Behind Mr. Adams, Captain Hunter emerged slowly from the cabin. He wore no coat, only his shirt and breeches, and the shirt was nearly as red as it was white. His face was deathly pale. "Sir!" I cried out, and ran to offer him support.

Captain Hunter's pale blue eyes seemed not to recognize me for a moment. Then he murmured, "I thank you, Davy."

My uncle said, "William—"

"In a moment, Patch," Captain Hunter said, sounding as if he were speaking in a dream. He patted my shoulder and then limped forward. I saw that he carried a prayer book.

The men in the waist and the forecastle paused, looking around at him. I wondered where Captain Barrel was, but then realized with a shock that one of the figures working on the broken bowsprit was Captain Barrel, stripped to the waist and with a scarf tied round his head. He slipped from the stump of the bowsprit to the deck and then limped on his wooden leg to meet Captain Hunter.

The captain leaned against the mainmast with one hand and raised his voice: "Men!" They all turned to him, silent and solemn. Captain Hunter held up the prayer book. "We have to bury our dead. I would read the service for each of them, but we have no time. Instead I will say only that we commend their bodies to the sea and their souls to God, who will surely understand."

"Amen," said Mr. Tate, who stood near the closest body.

"Go help them, Davy," said my uncle.

I hurried over to Mr. Tate. Together he and I lifted the heavy body to the rail. Mr. Tate hoarsely called out, "Matthew Parson, bosun's mate!"

The crew on deck returned, "Go with God!"

I felt my skin crinkle into gooseflesh. This was the old pirate's burial service: "Go with God," and a heave overboard.

Twelve times in all it was repeated, the naming of the dead and then that final splash. By the time we had finished, I was shaking with weariness and in reaction to all I had seen and done that day.

After the men had been fed, Uncle Patch insisted on treating Captain Hunter's wounds. "Do it in the cabin, then," the captain said peevishly, "for I have to learn from John Barrel what is what."

So it happened that I was in the cabin when my uncle ripped the bloody bandages from Captain Hunter's arm and side. His hurts were not fatal, but they must have made him sick with loss of blood. His shoulder wound took several stitches. His left biceps had been thrust through, and he panted and gasped as Uncle Patch sewed that gash together. A pistol or musket ball had scored his right side between his armpit and the bottom of his rib cage, and again that called for cleaning and stitching. "Faith," said my uncle with a grunt, "I believe ye have only a pint of blood left in you."

When he had been bandaged and dressed again, Captain Hunter asked Mr. Adams to bring in Captain Barrel. I sat in the corner, thinking that both my uncle and Captain Hunter looked as gaunt and as sallow as the dead. Captain Barrel, now wearing his shirt again, came stomping into the cabin. "How's it with ye, shipmate?" he asked.

"I'll do," Captain Hunter answered him. "Sit, Captain Barrel."

"Mighty obliged I am," said Captain Barrel, sinking into the armchair. "We've woolded the bowsprit. It'll serve until we can get to Cruzado. The *Fury* will take a mort o' carpenterin', too, but she's sound, she is."

Captain Hunter had some brandy brought in

and then asked, "How did you come to be prisoner on your own craft, Captain Barrel? You're not a man easily fooled."

Captain Barrel drank the brandy at one go, his face darkening. "I thought it was you, at first," he said. "We spied a sail, and closed on her. 'Twas the spit of the *Aurora,* from any distance—a black-and-yellow French-built frigate. She hailed us, an' I saw you—somebody dressed up like you, any gate, in a green-and-gold coat—on the quarterdeck. I figured ye wanted to gam, so I had some men row me across. No sooner did I put my timber toe onto that deck, than did somebody lay me low with a blow that put out my lights. When I come to again, I found the men from that ship had boarded the *Fury*. And who should be a-commandin' of the frigate but that bald-headed Satan, Shark."

"Aye," put in my uncle sharply. "The same man William shot in Tortuga."

"Did ye shoot him?" Captain Barrel asked, with a chuckle of delight. "Good for you, says I, and too bad your aim wasn't true! Aye, 'twas Shark, one o' Steele's chief lieutenants. Then it was I learned the ship was the *Janus,* near twin to this one here. That blasted dog told me to my face that was I friend to William Hunter, I was enemy to Jack Steele. And before I knowed it, he had me an' my loyal men in irons. We sailed that way for days. But ere long, I learnt from what few words the crew dropped that they was lookin' for the *Aurora*. They knowed your cruisin' grounds and knowed ye put in at Cruzado for repairs. They meant to do ye the same way they done me. Make ye think ye were approachin' the *Fury* an' friends, an' then kill ye if they could."

"So," my uncle said. "Well, well, William. I cannot say I approve of slaughter, for that would go against my training as a doctor. Still, you heaved Shark's body overboard, and I can but say good riddance to him!"

"So says I," added Captain Barrel. "Devil take his sorry soul!"

Captain Barrel excused himself to go back to the *Fury* and oversee repairs there. When we were alone, Captain Hunter stretched his bandaged arm and groaned. "Patch," he said, "I ask your pardon. I have been a right fool."

"Aye, that ye have," replied my uncle carelessly. Then, with his creaking laugh, he added, "But ye know it now. That's half the way back, William."

CHAPTER 9

Fever

WE SPENT JUST enough time in the harbor of the low Bahamian island of Cruzado to make the most-needed repairs. The pirate colony there had news of Jamaica: King James II had seen fit to send out a new governor for the island and to restore Sir Henry Morgan to the council. When he heard that, Captain Hunter said, "Then that decides me. Some of the men are suffering from wounds, and we've lost far too many to death. We'll sail to Sir Henry's plantation at Port Maria, on the north shore of Jamaica. I need his advice, and I need new recruits if we're to continue to pursue Steele."

The *Fury* had taken a far worse pounding than we

had and needed more repairs, but when John Barrel got wind of Captain Hunter's intentions, he came stomping aboard, hemmed and hawed, and finally came out with his intentions. "Which the boys an' me wants to ask Sir Henry for the king's pardon, now he's in good again. But we're naught but a skillington crew now, as ye might say. I'd take it kindly if we could sail in consort with the *Aurora*."

Captain Hunter readily agreed. After a few days of intense activity, and of great irritation because of the clouds of biting flies and mosquitoes that plagued Cruzado at that time of year, we had enough of a "lash-up," as Captain Barrel called the repairs, to set out. The winds were faint and contrary, and it looked to be a long sail to Port Maria, a matter of weeks or more, especially with the undermanned *Fury* struggling along in our wake.

We were not many days at sea when I awoke one morning with a dismally aching head. Breakfast was skilligalee, a thin porridge of oatmeal sweetened with molasses. We also had, at my uncle's insistence, cheese and fruit. My stomach lurched at the sight of the food, and I ate nothing, but sat shivering with a chill.

"Here," rumbled Uncle Patch, frowning from his side of the table. "What's this?"

I mumbled something, but he was out of his seat in an instant and leaning over me. He took my pulse, held back my eyelid, and peered at me with his emerald-green stare, then clapped a cool palm on my forehead.

Captain Hunter, from his seat, asked, "What is it?"

"Fever." My uncle, with no more ado, hurried me to the sick berth and into a hammock. He brought me a vile, bitter medicine, compounded of tree bark, and made me swallow it down. So began three or four of the worst days I spent aboard the *Aurora*.

By that evening, I ached in every joint and shivered with wave after wave of chills. I had no strength, and my uncle had to lift me from the hammock and hold a chamber pot for me so I could make water, as if I were a baby. I almost wept from the shame of it. He hoisted me back onto the hammock and told me to lie easy, but with the pains in my head and limbs, that I could not do.

I passed a terrible night, swallowed more nasty-tasting medicines, and somehow slipped into a very strange state, half dreaming and half awake. A hanging lantern with a solitary candle swung back and forth from a hook, giving me a dim light. As I stared up at the beams above my hammock, it seemed to me that one knot in the wood looked like an elephant. In truth I had never seen an elephant, but that was what I thought. And somehow, a whole parade of elephants lumbered across the sick berth and passed close by my hammock. In my fevered imagination they were great hoglike creatures, with flopping pointed ears like a pig's and a pig's snout, only three or four feet long. They had red, shaggy fur, and glared at me from small, mean eyes. One of them stopped, looked at me, and said, "Delirium," in my uncle's voice.

The next thing I truly knew was that I lay gasping and wet in the hammock, and my uncle was standing beside me. "And how is it with you, Davy?" he asked kindly.

"I'm soaking," I muttered. My cheeks flamed with embarrassment. "I didn't—"

"'Tis nothing but sweat," my uncle answered comfortingly. "A laudable sudation, as 'tis termed in medicine, a beneficial sweat. Your fever has broken, that's all. And now you've had it, you need never fear the yellow jack again."

From that moment I mended, learning that I was one of four aboard who had come down with yellow fever, or "yellow jack" as the sailors called it. I was first to recover, and was already helping my uncle in the sick berth again a few days later when Samuel Vetch, a maintopman, died of the fever, the whites of his eyes as yellow as an egg yolk. He was the only hand we lost. But on the very day I was myself again, my uncle brought John Barrel into the sick berth, ill with the disease. "Tell the lads t' sail back to Cruzado an' hole up," he groaned through chattering teeth. "If I live through this here yellow jack, I'll bring 'em word from Sir Henry."

And so the *Fury* turned back, with hardly enough sailors left aboard to sail her. Captain Barrel weathered the fever remarkably well, and after a few days he, too, was up and about, though weak. "You an' me, Davy lad," he said with a twisted grin, "we stared ol' Yellow Jack in his face, didn't we?"

"Aye," I answered. "And stared him down!"

"That we did!" And Captain Barrel roared with

laughter, slapping his thigh in his pleasure at having once more cheated death.

How many days we were at sea I no longer remember, but we raised the north coast of Jamaica at last and came in close to glide along within sight of the Blue Mountains, which looked cool and inviting to those of us sweltering through the days of a West Indian high summer. We passed a few craft, but no one hailed us or seemed in the least interested. Uncle Patch remarked that the north coast was a little wilder than Port Royal. "There's no need for a coat of blue paint here," he said. "So long as we anchor in some out-of-the-way spot and come quietly in to Port Maria."

Evening was closing in as the *Aurora* dropped anchor in the estuary of a small creek. I was to go ashore again, with Captain Hunter, my uncle, and John Barrel. Abel Tate readied the longboat, and we had four able-bodied seamen to row us in, around a headland and then into the port itself. We gathered on deck. I was wearing a brown suit that my uncle had bought for me a year and more before in Port Royal and was finding that it was now short in the arms and in the legs. My uncle was decently dressed in the black he favored as befitting a doctor. He also wore a simple gray wig, probably to hide the spot on the side of his head where at last he had consented to allow Mr. Grice to shave his wound and put a few neat, small stitches in the gash. It was healing well, but the bristly shaved spot looked odd.

Captain Hunter wore his gorgeous green coat, though he had settled on a more modest hat than the one with an ostrich plume that he wore from time to time. "Do I not look the image of a wealthy merchant?" he asked.

In a dry tone, my uncle answered him. "Or a pirate king, as played on the boards of a provincial theater!"

"Ready, gents?" asked a rough voice, and John Barrel hoisted himself up through a grating. "I asked a man to barber me, an' he found me this here coat, which I hope I may borrow for the occasion."

I must have gawped like an openmouthed fish. Captain Barrel had had his beard trimmed short so that it no longer fell in kinked bunches halfway to his waist, and his long dark hair was tied back. In a decent blue coat that probably belonged to my uncle, for it was far too large in the shoulders for

Captain Hunter, he looked nearly respectable.

We glided into the harbor, exciting no attention, and quickly found our way to the plantation house owned by Sir Henry. Captain Barrel fidgeted like an embarrassed boy as we stood on the verandah and knocked on the door. A servant opened it, and Captain Hunter sent a note in to the master of the house. The servant allowed us into the entryway before vanishing down a hall. Moments later we heard quick footsteps, and then to my astonishment Miss Helena Fairfax emerged from a passageway, a candlestick in her hand.

"It really is you!" she said with a delighted smile.

"It is enchanting to see you again," answered the captain with a deep bow. "But surprising! How came you to be here?"

"I came with my granduncle, Sir Reginald, who is a member of the council," she said. "This way, gentlemen."

She showed us into a parlor, where a tall, bony old man sat in a fancy chair. A bottle of wine and a glass stood on a round table at his elbow, and I could see pretty well the symptoms of some determined drinking on his face. But he rose, and he greeted us with a polite smile and not the least slurring of his speech.

Before Miss Fairfax could speak, the captain bowed again and said, "Sir Reginald, I understand. I am Captain Hunt, with some business for Sir Henry. Permit me to introduce my friend Mr. Patrick, and Mr. Barr, a fellow sea captain."

"Pleasure," murmured Sir Reginald. "I believe Sir Henry will be available shortly. My dear niece, do you mind playing the hostess? I am somewhat fatigued and was just going up to bed."

"Not at all, Uncle," said Miss Fairfax.

I noticed that Sir Reginald took his bottle of wine with him. "My uncle is a very discreet man when he wants to be," Miss Fairfax confided. "Now, Captain, you must tell me of your adventures."

"They are hardly fit for your ears," said Captain Hunter with a shake of his head.

"Must I be disappointed? Very well, then. Let me show you to Sir Henry's study. He should be with you shortly."

She took us to a spacious room with a desk, a long mahogany table, and plenty of chairs, and there she took her leave of us. But we were not alone for long. I heard slow, heavy footsteps in the hall, the door swung open, and Sir Henry Morgan, the old buccaneer himself, stepped into the room. He threw his head back and laughed, and then said, "Blast my eyes! Old John Barrel, in the flesh! They haven't hung you yet, man?"

Captain Barrel had not taken a seat. He laughed too and limped forward on his timber leg to give Sir Henry a hearty handshake. "No, Your Honor," he said. "They've shot me an' they've cut me an' beat me an' chained me, but nobody's hung me yet. Not 'less ye plans to do it now!"

"Sit, sit," said Morgan, and he collapsed into his own chair at the big desk. Only then did I notice how pale and ill he looked. He was a big man, but he seemed to have lost weight everywhere but in his belly, which looked swollen. And my uncle stirred at the sound of Morgan's heavy, labored breathing. After a few seconds, Morgan tilted his head at Captain Hunter. "You've done pretty well, William. I suppose you need help, though."

"I'll not hide it from you, Sir Henry," Captain Hunter told him. "I'm short of hands and short of hope, and look to you for a new supply of both."

Morgan nodded. "Sawbones?"

"Faith," muttered my uncle. "I came but to see whether you've been taking your medicine and staying to your diet. And one glimpse of you tells me you have not!"

With a wave of his hand, Morgan said, "I have other doctors. They are treating me." With a gleam in his eye, he turned to Captain Barrel. "And you, old shipmate?"

Captain Barrel coughed. "Well, Your Honor, we've had word that you're back in favor. Me an' the lads were hoping ye might have a king's pardon about ye."

Morgan shook with rumbling laughter. "By the Powers! I never thought the day would come. D'ye stand there, John Barrel, and tell me you're turning honest?"

With a shrug, Captain Barrel answered, "Aye! I'll tell ye the truth, Morgan. I've sailed for the devil hisself, or for Jack Steele, which amounts to the same. What have I got for it? My ship stove in, an' me clapped in irons by that swab that called hisself Shark. Shiver me timbers, but if Steele treats me such a way, why, I won't say no to sailin' for King

James. After Steele, Lusty Charlie's boy will be a step up."

Morgan sat silent for a little space. Then he opened a drawer, withdrew from it a piece of parchment, and reached for a quill pen. He dipped it in ink and signed the document, then sprinkled sand onto the fresh ink. He blew this off carelessly, waved the parchment, and passed it over to Barrel. "There's your pardon, John Barrel. And I hope you and your men have learned your lesson."

"That we have," said Captain Barrel with a wide grin. "Ye have my affydavy on that!"

Sir Henry took two or three deep breaths, and my uncle leaped from his place. "Let me feel your pulse, sir!" he ordered.

"I'll be well enough," Morgan said, shaking his head. "William, you need men and you need hope, you say. I can help you with the former. I think my other guest may help you with the latter." He raised his voice and called, "Miss Fairfax!"

She opened the door an instant later, and I realized she had been waiting in the adjoining room. "Yes, Sir Henry?"

Morgan gave Captain Hunter a strange, sly smile.

"You may show His Excellency in now, my dear," he told Miss Fairfax.

She disappeared back into the other room, and I heard her murmuring voice. And then something beyond astonishing happened.

Don Esteban de Reyes, the Spanish captain who once had vowed to kill Captain Hunter, stepped into the room.

CHAPTER 10

Deal with the Devil

"I BELIEVE YOU know everyone here, Your Excellency?" Morgan rumbled in the sudden silence. I have heard about it being so quiet you could hear a pin drop, but I'd never experienced it until that very moment. No one spoke, no one moved. No one even breathed.

Don Esteban de Reyes, the captain and owner of the dread Spanish pirate hunter ship *Concepcíon,* stared back at us, the slightest of smiles on his face. He was a short, stocky dark man in a plain black uniform with a single silver starburst on the right breast. The sword at his side was unadorned and serviceable.

"Pity I went to all the trouble o' patchin' the captain up, Davy," my uncle muttered next to me, "just to have it all to do again."

Out of the corner of my eye, I could see both Captain Hunter and Captain Barrel slowly moving their hands toward their swords. Don Esteban casually raised one eyebrow and they both stopped. There was something heavy and methodical about the stocky Don, and both the captains were still recovering from their wounds taken in defense of the *Aurora*. Yet even if they had been in prime shape, I do not think they could have easily taken Don Esteban. Finally he nodded slightly in acknowledgment of Sir Henry's question.

"Yes, Sir Henry, I do know everyone in this room, at least by reputation."

"By the Powers, Harry," Captain Barrel exploded. "Have ye taken leave of your senses? Have ye no idea of who this be?"

"Of course I know who it is!" Sir Henry roared like a wounded lion. "I make it a habit to know everyone I invite into me own house! And that's Sir Henry to you, John Barrel, you old reprobate!"

During this exchange, Captain Hunter was

working to overcome his shock. A grim smile finally touched his lips, and he made a curt bow in the direction of the Spaniard, though his hand stayed close to his sword. "A good evening to you, Don Esteban. I had hoped to make your acquaintance one day, though this is sooner than I had expected."

"Life is full of little surprises, Captain Hunter."

"This is ever so entertaining," snapped Miss Fairfax with a note of exasperation in her voice. "But I suggest you gentlemen make yourselves comfortable so that Sir Henry can tell you of his plan. I shall see to some wine—assuming my dear uncle has left any!" And with that, she swept from the room, radiating contempt for every man since Adam named the animals.

"A very formidable young woman," said Don Esteban, sighing.

"You, sir, do not know the half of it," agreed Captain Hunter.

"Then I suggest you all take your seats," snapped Sir Henry, gesturing toward the great table in the center of the room and the ornate chairs around it. "Don Esteban and I have been parleying for a reason.

Now that you are all here, I want you to share in the talk. I care not for what has gone before or what will come after! Now we have need of one another!"

"It is not easy to set aside deep differences just for convenience's sake, Sir Henry," Don Esteban said in a cold, flat voice, not taking his eyes from Captain Hunter, who coldly nodded back. With a collapsing rumble, Morgan slowly settled into his own great chair.

"Aye, there is a difference, Your Excellency. I have presented you with ample evidence that it was not Captain Hunter and the *Aurora* who sacked poor little San Angel. If you were not convinced, you would not be here. The truth of it is, sir, we all have blood enough on our hands to paint this room red. But another man has enough to fill it. So the question is what is more important? Your differences or putting an end to Jack Steele?"

Once again the room was deadly quiet. Then Captain Hunter took his hand away from his sword, pulled out an ornately carved chair, and sat himself down at Sir Henry Morgan's table. Don Esteban hesitated but a second longer and then he, too, drew out a chair and sat down.

"Oh, well, in for a penny, in for a pound," grumbled my uncle, and he and John Barrel also sat down.

"Well begun is half done," Sir Henry said, taking another long, deep breath. "First, let us share a bit of information. I have not spent the last months simply ignoring your advice, Doctor Shea. I have been at work gathering information. The two of you dealt Jack Steele a grand defeat at Tortuga. You smashed the independent Brotherhood of the Coast before they could join up with the *Red Queen*. But you didn't put a finish to him!" He settled back into his chair, suddenly looking pale and clammy. "Now I have new word, and I am almost sure I know what he plans to do."

"You have all our attention, Sir Henry," said the dark Spaniard.

Sir Henry nodded. "Then listen closely, for it covers all of us. Ships are disappearing. Ships are being looted and stripped. The monster is picking up the pieces you two left floating about. Ships and captains and crews. This time it's no league made up of gentlemen o' fortune. He's building his own navy. He's buying ships that will sail under the command of their very own pirate admiral!"

A servant had softly entered the room and was quietly placing glasses of deep red wine in front of everyone. He was ignored.

Sir Henry spread his hands on the table. "If he'd succeeded at Tortuga, Steele would have commanded fifty motley vessels. Instead he will now command a tight fleet of twenty, with the bloody *Red Queen* herself to lead them on! He means to take territory, Captain Hunter, mark my words. Make himself king o' Jamaica or some such."

"How can a man be so mad and so cunning, all at once?" asked my uncle in a wondering voice.

"He's a remarkable villain," Sir Henry countered. "We know so much about the pirate but so little about the man." He took a sip of wine and gasped for air. Then roughly he said, "Been lookin' into that, too. We think he was a merchant from out of Plymouth by the name of Jonathan Steele. Well respected he was, had a wife and a daughter and a good business dealing in soaps and perfumes and such."

"Jack Steele was a perfumer?" said John Barrel, amazement in every word.

"So we think. Then he and his family set out on

one of his ships for the Virginia colony. Never made it. She vanished as completely as if she'd never been built. Months later, someone like him took a sloop and massacred everyone who wouldn't join him, and that was the birth of Jack Steele. Something happened out there on the high seas. Something terrible. I haven't been able to find out what it was, but it turned an anonymous little merchant into a cold and calculating killing machine."

I stood quiet in the shadows, taking in everything Sir Henry was saying. There had been something— no, some*one*—before the monster who was Jack Steele. And like Sir Henry, I found myself wondering what could have happened to make so startling a change in a man.

"So life dealt him a rough hand," growled John Barrel. "Life's hard, an' that's that. But where the devil did Steele get his hands on that ship o' his? Sixty guns she had to begin with, an' she's got a powerful sight more'n that now. Big 'uns, too. But where the devil did he get her, that's what I wants to know."

"Ah, well," murmured Don Esteban, finally taking a sip of his wine. "I fear that's our fault."

Everyone turned to stare at him. He sighed. "You will be the first English to hear this tale; it is not one the Royal Court particularly wants spread about."

"I can't wait to hear this," said my uncle to John Barrel as he eased back into his chair. Captain Barrel nodded his agreement and also settled back.

Don Esteban sighed again. "There was a commission made to the shipbuilders of Holland to construct a gigantic merchant galleon for the flota."

"Spanish treasure fleet," said Captain Barrel, nodding wisely at me, though I already knew what the flota was.

"Yes, Captain Barrel, the great silver fleet that sails once a year for Spain. She was the *Sangreal*, the Holy Grail, much larger than most of her class and heavily armed. However, she was storm damaged in her first crossing and was sent to Havana Harbor for repairs. It was there, one dark night after the repair work was completed, that she was boarded and her caretaker crew slaughtered, their bodies tossed overboard. Before the garrisons in the great castles guarding the harbor became aware of what had happened, she had set sail and slipped away into the night."

"So the notorious *Red Queen* is just a tricked-up treasure galleon with a bit of meat on her bones?" Captain Hunter frowned even as he said the words.

"That is nonsense, sir," snapped a soft voice from the doorway. Miss Fairfax had returned and stood there glaring. "I might remind you, Don Esteban, that I have seen the *Red Queen,* and she is no more any kind of merchant ship than the *Aurora* or the *Concepcíon.*"

"And I saw her once from a distance," said Captain Hunter. "It was a short enough glimpse, for she fired on us and all but sank us. But she had not the lines of a galleon."

"She has not, Captain Hunter, not any longer. And you are right, my lady. The *Red Queen* is not any more the *Sangreal.* She has been changed."

"Well, I am profoundly confused," said my uncle cheerfully, throwing his hands up in the air. "Treasure ship, warship, fish, or fowl . . . what is she, exactly?"

Don Esteban gave him a long, dark look. "The great treasure galleon is no more, Doctor Shea. What is in her place is, as you said, neither fish nor fowl. There is nothing like the *Red Queen* anywhere on the

Seven Seas. Captain Steele completely altered her."
The Spaniard turned to Captain Hunter. "Tell me,
sir, what do you know of the *Red Queen*?"

Captain Hunter frowned. "What everyone knows,
I suppose. She's oversized, she's bloodred. I saw her
only once. She is monstrously large, and strangely
fast."

"Few have done as you. Few have seen her and
lived to tell of it. And fewer still would be believed.
Steele took her to one of his hidden bases. Then he
ripped her apart and rebuilt her to some plan of his
own. He razed the forecastle by one deck and the
aftercastle by two. No galleon has ever had lines so
low."

"Better stability, though" rumbled Morgan. "The
curse of the galleons, and I mean no offense, Don
Esteban, is that they tower so high that the wind
catches 'em. They make shocking leeway."

"Not when ballasted with gold and silver,"
returned the Spanish captain.

"How do you know all this, Don Esteban?" asked
Captain Hunter.

For the first time, Don Esteban looked uncomfortable. "We were able to capture one of the men who

worked on the transformation. He was . . . persuaded to provide information." Don Esteban closed his eyes and began to recite like a schoolboy doing his lessons. "The *Red Queen* is one hundred and eighty feet long. Her gun decks have been increased from two to three. A year ago, her armament was sixty sixteen-pound cannons. That has changed. Now her lower deck carries twenty-four thirty-two pounders; her middle deck carries thirty-four twenty-four pounders; her upper deck carries sixteen sixteen pounders. There are two nine-pound bow-chasers and four stern chasers of the same size. Her crew is approximately four hundred and twenty-five."

The silence that followed this list of statistics was absolute. I stood in my corner with my mouth open just like all the adults seated around the table. Eighty guns. That was as many as a ship of the line could carry.

"No, no, that is just not possible," my uncle objected.

"One hundred and eighty feet?" wondered Captain Hunter. "The *Aurora*'s but one hundred."

"And the *Concepcion* is but one forty," finished Don Esteban.

"Now do you understand, Captain Hunter?" said Miss Fairfax, hugging herself as she sat in the corner. "The *Red Queen* isn't a ship, she's a monster, a nightmare with sails. And she and the madman who created her are drawing others to her side!"

"Aye," breathed John Barrel. "My bonnie *Fury* would serve her as a longboat, so she would."

"You see how it is, gentlemen," said a strangely shrunken Sir Henry Morgan. "There can be precious little help from the Royal Navy in this case. King James has troubles of his own right now and I think I spill no secrets when I say there are no more than four navy ships in these waters."

"Your news would be more interesting if Spain had more ships," agreed Don Esteban. "I believe the French and the Dutch are in much the same situation. And none of them could stand up against the *Red Queen*."

"So it comes down to this," Captain Hunter said, staring off into space. "We—the men around this table—must find the *Red Queen*'s last secret base and destroy it. And her. And Captain Jack Steele." He turned his stare to Don Esteban. "To do that we must cooperate, all differences forgotten, until that great task is finished. Or the sea of the Caribbees is a pirate lake and Jack Steele is its king forever."

Don Esteban closed his eyes and we all held our breath. He had fought beside us once before but his commission, like ours, was to hunt pirates, and he considered us pirates. Every other Spaniard in the New World thought we were the butchers of San Angel. Had Sir Henry's evidence convinced him of our innocence?

Finally that slight smile appeared again on the dark Spaniard's face. "Our course is clear and only fools would try to sail against it. But you must forgive me, Captain Hunter, if I say it is too perilously close to making a deal with the devil himself."

Gravely he offered his hand, and just as gravely Captain Hunter shook it.

And there in the grand study of Sir Henry Morgan's great plantation house did the English and Spanish pirate hunters once again join forces to fight the greatest pirate of them all.

Jack Steele and the bloody *Red Queen*.

CHAPTER 11

The Unlikely Armada

ON THE SIMMERING first day of August 1688, under the lightest of breezes, the *Aurora* glided through the waters south of Cayo Hueso, the last island in a long chain curving down from the Spanish territory of Florida. I was finding life aboard the ship strange again, for Sir Henry had delivered to us new recruits, and our crew was one hundred and eighty strong once more. But so many new faces made me feel ill at ease, as if distant relatives had moved into my home, and me not knowing a one of them.

High, streaky clouds painted themselves across a deep blue sky. Mr. Tate, who was an old hand in these waters, said they were omens of a hurricane out in the Atlantic. One of the new men cursed him and his omens, warning him not even to talk of such storms. "Namin' bad luck calls it, ye know," the ill-natured stranger growled. Mr. Tate shrugged it off as a sailor's superstition.

We were to sail within sight of the low island until the others joined us. Mercifully both vessels did on the second day, and that meant we could hoist sail and get under way, finding some relief from the heat. In this place the sun that beat straight down at noon turned the pitch in the seams between the deck boards into black, sticky liquid.

By sunset of the second day of August the *Concepción* and the *Fury* had come within hailing distance, and all that night we cast our course east-ward, to weather the east point of Cuba and then turn southward, ranging past Jamaica and from there down to Yucatan and points south. The next day, both Don Esteban and Captain Barrel came aboard, and we all huddled in the cabin.

"Tell them what you heard in the tavern, Davy," Captain Hunter instructed.

I did so, mentioning the drunken sailor's

mumblings about Bloodhaven. "He said Steele would be there or at San Angel," I finished.

"He certainly had been at San Angel," my uncle put in dryly.

"Bloodhaven?" muttered Captain Barrel. "Either of ye gents know where it might lie?"

"It is not on any chart," Don Esteban declared.

"I've never even heard of it," added Captain Hunter.

"Aye, there's the wonder of it all," Captain Barrel observed. "Devil a pirate I've ever seen as runs such a tight-knit crew as Steele's. They be afeard o' him, and that's part of it. But a bigger part is loyalty. The man commands his crew's loyalty like . . . like a blessed admiral."

"And he slaughters those loyal to him just to trap an enemy," my uncle said. "We saw what he did to San Angel."

"Bloodhaven, now," Captain Barrel continued, without paying much heed to Uncle Patch's interruption. "To be sure, I've heard of it, but just in a general way, as ye might say. It be somewhere on the Spanish Main, belike. It could lie anywhere between Portobello an' Cozumel, for that matter. Might be one of the Miskitas, or might lie near Old Providence, both on 'em prime pirate hideaways at one time."

"Someone will know," Captain Hunter assured him. "I'm positive that Steele has a safe haven somewhere. He cannot sail in and out without being spied by someone. We will ask fishermen, traders, anyone we see. Sooner or later we shall find him, mark my words."

A day or two later, we caught the tail end of the blow Mr. Tate had foreseen. It was rough weather, with gales of wind and black lashings of rain ripping the sea to gray-white foam that flew away like ghosts. The *Aurora* plunged and rose and bucked and groaned, even under only a staysail to give us headway. We lost touch with the other two craft. This was the kind of weather that had made me seasick before, and so it did a few of our old hands. More than once I saw a sailor step lively to the rail, lean over, and throw up to leeward, afterward wiping his mouth in a businesslike way and going straight back to work, as if nothing remarkable had happened.

I found that I was less sick on deck than belowdecks, so I spent much of the storm near the helmsmen, for it took two of them when the weather was rough. Once I recall the poor ship had climbed up a swelling, green, foam-streaked mountain of a wave. We balanced on the crest of it for a moment, with the wind shrieking in the rigging and rain coming horizontal, hitting as hard as musket balls. Then the bow dipped and we plunged down into the trough of the wave in a sickening, rushing dip that was only just short of falling.

I held on to something—a backstay, the rail, I do not remember—and watched with sick fascination. As we rushed downward, the waves cut off the wind, and suddenly the howling in the rigging ceased, leaving only the dismal universal roar of the storm. To my horror, the bow of the *Aurora* stabbed into the sea, as if we were heading down to the bottom, and for a moment I was sure we would never rise. One of the men at the whipstaff cried out, "God save us!"

And then with a terrible, creaking groan, the good ship raised her bow again, and a green wall of water came washing straight back along the deck. It smacked into me chest-high, and I felt my feet sweep from under me. For a moment only my death grip on the backstay and the rail held me aboard, and then the water poured from the scuppers as if we had taken a waterfall aboard us. And then we were climbing one of those monstrous waves again.

By the time the storm had passed, we had much mending to do, but nothing had carried away or broken. With a fresher wind, we found our two consorts. Neither of them was badly damaged, and together the three of us fairly flew to the south.

That was just the beginning of dreary weeks spent coasting along. We met precious few vessels, and none of them had any news to share. Sometimes we threaded our way through a maze of low islands or ghosted along northward within sight of the coast of Central America, praying that no strong wind would spring up to wreck us, for the chief of a sailor's fears is to be caught on a lee shore, a shore toward which a strong wind is blowing. In such cases, a ship has small hope of surviving, and so does her crew.

We were nearing the territory of Yucatan by the

first of September. That afternoon Mr. Adams and I slaved away at our mathematical studies on deck, for the heat below was stifling. Mr. Adams's mathematical studies had fairly blossomed. Somehow understanding had taken root within him, and he was now showing me how to work hard problems in trigonometry. Lord knows, it could not have been my uncle's teaching that made the difference, for he knew as much of the higher mathematics as a flounder does of the Alps. Perhaps it was simply that Mr. Adams had grown desperate, and desperation drove him to great effort.

At any rate, late that night I lay in my hammock, dripping with sweat and vainly trying to sleep. At last I gave up and swung down to the deck. My uncle, in his cot, was snoring away, for he could drop off at any time and in any place. I took a pillow and went up on deck to find a coil of rope where I might curl up in the relative coolness.

It must have been well past midnight when a hurried exchange of voices woke me up. "To the north, see?" someone said. "Better tell the cap'n."

I sprang up. "What is it?"

One of the new men jumped a foot, swore, and then said, "The loblolly boy? What're you doin' above boards?"

"Hush up, Sweeney," said the other, a man I knew to be Obedience Jackson. "He's our mascot, like. He brings us good luck."

By then I had heard what had drawn their attention. It was a low, distant rumble, something like thunder. But it was not thunder, for I had heard the sound often before. Somewhere to the north, a ship was firing its guns.

I sprang to the rigging and clambered up to the maintop, where Olaf Petersen gave me a grunting welcome. "Ye can see there, about three points to larboard. Watch steady."

Presently I did see flashes—or rather the red reflection of flashes—far in the distance. Long seconds later the thundery sound rolled in again. "Shall I tell Captain Hunter?" I asked, knowing that the two sailors below were still uncertain.

"As ye see fit," Mr. Petersen told me. I slid down a backstay, hardly thinking twice about it, and landed softly on my bare feet. I hurried aft and tapped on the captain's door.

Captain Hunter opened it, holding aloft a lantern. "Davy! What the devil?"

"Gunfire, sir, to the north. Perhaps seven leagues or more away, three points off the windward bow."

Captain Hunter was in his breeches and shirt. He paused only to pull on a pair of slippers and then hurried onto the deck. "Masthead, there!" he bawled, with his hand cupped beside his mouth. "What do you see?"

"Flashes o' fire," Mr. Petersen responded. "I make it to be two vessels."

The captain checked our speed, a bare two knots. At that rate, it might take us eight or ten hours to get to the scene of the fight. He called the watch aloft and spread more canvas, and our speed increased to a trifle over four knots, but with the wind we had, that was the best we could do. The *Fury* and the *Concepcion* were nowhere near, though we had an appointment to rendezvous with them a few days later. Whatever we found to the north, we would have to deal with it alone.

Somehow I slept some that night. The wind picked up a bit, and by dawn we had made about eighteen good sea miles of progress. The firing had long since fallen silent, though Mr. Petersen had reported that he saw a red glare for a long time, as if a ship had been set afire.

In the first gray light of day someone spied a body. It was a sailor, and he had been dead for at least a few hours. His injuries looked as though cannon fire had inflicted them. We passed him by, abandoning him to a school of small sharks. Before long we saw more debris: a floating cask, a splintered yardarm. The *Aurora* traced a zigzag path across the seas until finally the lookout, no longer Mr. Petersen but another man, shouted down that he saw a boat.

We closed on it. It proved to be no boat at all, but rather a kind of raft of casks, a chicken coop, and some planks, all tangled together with ropes. And on it lay a body that stirred feebly. Six of us went into one of the gigs and rowed over to him. He was a youngish man, perhaps twenty, with grievous wounds in his abdomen. He was scarcely conscious as we hauled him aboard and carried him to the sick berth.

Uncle Patch shook his head the moment he had examined the man, but he set to work stitching and bandaging. The sailor began to groan as we worked on him, and at length he rasped, "I thought I was dead for sure. What ship is this, mate?"

"'Tis the ship that fished you out of the ocean, and that's all ye need know right now," answered my uncle. "Who might you be?"

"Name is Samuel Walters," he said. "I can't feel my legs at all."

"You have some bad wounds."

Walters licked his lips and lay still as my uncle tied off the last of the bandages. "Be I goin' to make it?" he asked.

For a long moment Uncle Patch looked into his face. Then in a soft voice he said, "If I were you, Samuel Walters, I would prepare to meet my Maker."

Walters winced. Then he growled, "So that's the way of it, is it? Curse Jack Steele!"

I cried out in surprise, but Uncle Patch shushed me. "What of Jack Steele?" he asked. "What have you to do with him?"

In a fading voice Walters said, "I were third mate in the *Janus*. Oh, she were a sweet-sailing French-built frigate, but Steele sunk her from under us." He trailed off.

My uncle gently shook his shoulder. "Tell me now, is that the ship that masqueraded as the *Aurora*?"

"Aye," said Walters. "Shark was our cap'n. But he died, so we heard tell from some o' his crew that come back from th' *Fury*. That were a sloop—"

"Yes, we know about her," my uncle said urgently.

Walters frowned. "It's main dark in here."

"It will be lighter by and by," Uncle Patch said. "What happened aboard the *Janus*?"

"Why, we elected a new cap'n, Ben Rogers, an' we come to rendezvous with the *Red Queen*. Rogers, he went over to report, an' next thing we on the *Janus* sees is Steele a-throwin' Ben's body overboard. Then he give the order to open up on us. We ran, and he chased all night. But he sank us at last."

Walters was drawing breath very hard. My uncle leaned close and said, "You're going out, Walters. But you can still do some good here. Where is Bloodhaven?"

"Daren't tell," Walters groaned. "It's so dark in here."

We had four lanterns burning, and the wind port let daylight in.

"Hang it, man," Uncle Patch said intensely, "this

is the *Aurora*. Do you understand that? We're looking for Steele, and we mean to send him to the bottom. You'll be beyond Steele's reach in a few minutes. Where is Bloodhaven?"

"Be I goin'?" asked Walters in a whisper. He took a deep breath and held it so terribly long I thought he had died. But then he exhaled. "Nineteen eighteen," he said so quietly I could hardly hear him.

Uncle Patch seized a scalpel and carved the numbers into a beam. Walters whispered more, numbers in the eighties. Then he said, "Longitude and latitude. Bloodhaven." And with that his throat rattled, and he died.

We made our rendezvous with the *Fury* and the *Concepción* the day after we buried Samuel Walters. And then we made our way toward the spot he had named, all sailing within sight of one another. We coasted northward along a shore rich with poisonous green vegetation. For the first time I began to be aware of how vast were the Spanish holdings in the New World, so huge that whole great sections of it still were hardly explored and could easily be all but invisible to those who governed it from far-off Spain.

Leaning on the rail and staring at the shore, Uncle Patch observed sourly, "I don't know what else we may find there, but I'll bet my teeth we shall find fever. I don't like the looks of this place, Davy, that I don't."

And day by day he grew grimmer as the ships glided ever closer to the location of Bloodhaven.

CHAPTER 12

The Secret Base

IT WAS THE FIFTEENTH of September when we finally arrived at the coordinates poor Samuel Walters had given us. There we discovered that what he had sworn to was true. Like ancient Celtic warriors from one of Uncle Patch's stories we had come to the end of our quest.

We lay anchored off the fairway that led into Bloodhaven.

"Anchor us firm and fair, Mr. Adams," Captain Hunter called out. "We're in tricky shoal water. Rocks down there'd rip the bottom out of the *Fury,* let alone the *Concepcion.*"

"How does something as big as the *Red Queen* is

supposed to be get in and out of here?" I asked my uncle as we stared over the *Aurora*'s side at the dark green shoreline.

"Sure, and he probably has it all mapped to a fare-thee-well, lad," he grumbled back. "Probably as clear as Bristol Walk if you know the way. He does, we don't, so we wait here."

And so we did in the sweltering heat, the nimble little *Fury* to our starboard, the great towering *Concepcion* to our port. The captains of our strange little armada had made plans for this. In the steaming night, four small boats slipped away from our ships and disappeared into the darkness. They were equally filled with former buccaneers and grim Spanish Marines. I would not have wanted to cross the wake of either of them, come dark or daylight.

We waited, and the heat came and went in waves, the night cool only in comparison to the day. The air was thick with the stench of dead fish and rotting vegetation. Even the water seemed to be dyed green, as if the sun had melted the thick growths along the shore and poured their slick hues into the sea. I had never realized what an ugly color green could be. Finally when it seemed as though we would soon all drown in our own sweat, a small triangular sail appeared, beating its way back to us. A crimson-and-gold banner fluttered from its single mast. Some of Don Esteban's marines had at last come back to report.

Soon I found myself standing beside Uncle Patch in the amazingly expansive captain's cabin on board the *Concepcion*. I remembered how poor John Barrel had complained about how William Hunter "had done himself well" with the *Aurora*'s cabin and furnishings. He stood next to Captain Hunter now, his mouth gaping open in frank covetousness. The cabin was huge, all dark wood and somber gilt. A tapestry covered one wall and depicted a towering galleon blowing some other vessel to pieces. I tried not to look too closely at the flag of the defeated ship. Don Esteban stood on the other side of a great round table, dressed as ever in his grim black uniform. Captain Hunter, in a quest for contrast, I suppose, was resplendent in his green coat and yellow sash. This time he had brought his ostrich plume hat but kept it discreetly under his arm.

Next to Don Esteban stood a powerfully built man with the blackest mustache I had ever seen. He stood at attention and glared at us. Don Esteban, on the other hand, actually smiled. "Welcome, gentlemen, to my humble quarters."

"Humble quarters," rumbled John Barrel. "I robbed from churches ain't half this grand." Don Esteban acted as though he hadn't heard anything, but I believe his smile grew slightly wider.

"This stalwart gentleman to my left is Sergeant Gonzalez, who was in command of the marines we sent ashore. He has returned to make his report." He glanced at the grim marine. "Sergeant?"

Stiff as a stringed puppet, the sergeant removed a roll of canvas from under his arm and spread it out on the table. We all crowded around it. It was a surprisingly detailed map of a harbor and a town. He said something in Spanish.

With a nod, Don Esteban said, "Sergeant Gonzalez is a man of many talents, not the least of which is a gift for the drawing of maps. Unfortunately his talents do not include a knowledge of any language but his own. With your kind permission, I shall translate." Don Esteban spoke in Spanish to the sergeant, who nodded.

Gonzalez pointed at the map, took a deep breath, and began to speak in a sharp, no-nonsense flow of Spanish. True to his word as ever, his captain spoke almost at the same time.

"Bloodhaven is here. A narrow harbor at the mouth of a small river. It is probably the only anchorage for ships of any real size for one hundred miles in any direction. It is because of this isolation that it has not been discovered by any of the legitimate authorities." A stiff finger stabbed down at the map. "The actual settlement is small but tight. The wharves are well constructed and extensive. The only stone buildings in the settlement proper are these four long structures here behind the piers. They are warehouses, except for the largest one, which has thicker walls and serves as an arsenal and powder magazine. The living quarters are situated behind the warehouses and for the most part are open-walled sleeping platforms with thatched roofs to keep off the sun and rain." The stocky marine rumbled to a stop, eyes staring straight ahead.

"The ships, Sergeant?" Don Esteban prodded softly.

The sergeant took another deep breath, and again as he spoke Don Esteban translated: "There are at this time twelve ships within the harbor. Their last locations are indicated on the chart. There are seven brigs, three sloops, and two pinnaces. All are armed and fully fitted to sail. Alas, there is no sign of the *Red Queen* or her evil captain."

I doubted that Sergeant Gonzalez had actually said the word "alas," but the effect of his translated words on Captain Hunter was alarming.

"Not here!" he snarled. "Steele not here! Will there never be an end to him?"

"Ease yourself, my friend," purred Don Esteban. "The rest of the good sergeant's tale will, if I am not mistaken, put Steele's absence more to our liking."

Sweat was beginning to break out on the sergeant's brow. I do not think he was used to public speaking. Once again the translation began. "There are two rocky islands, only a few acres in size, that lie just off the coast. One is two hundred yards south of the harbor entrance, the other a little farther north of it. Although they cannot be seen from the ocean, both islands contain fortifications cleverly constructed from native stone and planted with vines to obscure their lines." The sergeant's finger stabbed out again, quickly indicating positions on the map. "However, each one is armed with six forty-two-pound cannons, as well as smaller weapons. They are arranged so as to command a total crossfire of the only approach to the inner harbor."

"Forty-two pounders!" my uncle burst out. "Even the Royal Navy can't get forty-two pounders! Where does he steal this stuff from?"

"I doubt he steals it at all, Patch," said Captain Hunter, shaking his head. "He probably buys it from good English businessmen or some of the navy's more enterprising quartermasters. Lord only knows, after ten years of piracy he should have enough gold for it."

"*Gracias,* Sergeant," said Don Esteban, drawing us all back to the matter at hand. Sergeant Gonzalez actually sagged before settling into a position of rigid attention. His captain turned and smiled his blunt predator's smile.

"I would like to propose the following plan, gentlemen. My marines will land on the islands under the cover of darkness and take the forts. I suggest that a second party, composed of members of your inestimable crews, infiltrate Bloodhaven and set fires. As soon as the marines possess the forts, they will open fire on the ships at anchor in the harbor. The *Concepcion,* the *Aurora,* and the redoubtable *Fury* will stand off the approaches. When the ships that the forts do not sink try to break for the sea, we shall cut them down. All will be done before the *Red Queen* returns to discover her spawn dead and drowned."

Captain Hunter nodded solemnly as he contemplated Don Esteban's plan. John Barrel looked likely to burst with pride over the Spanish captain's description of his little craft as redoubtable. When first we met him, the *Fury* was trying to hold the *Concepcion* off while two other pirate ships burned around her. John Barrel and his crew were nothing if not brave. Captain Hunter nodded one more time and also pointed at the map.

"A solid plan, Your Excellency, most well thought out. However, I have a refinement that might serve us well. Let my men make the first move, let them take and set fire to the powder magazine your sergeant has pinpointed for us. When it goes up, it not only will take half of Bloodhaven with it, but also is sure to distract the garrisons at the forts. That will serve as your marines' signal to attack, for the men within are going to be gaping at the destruction ashore."

Not a word was said, but after a moment's contemplation Don Esteban bowed his head slightly in agreement. He murmured rapidly in Spanish, and the grim Sergeant Gonzalez slowly began to smile, exposing blindingly white teeth.

I shivered. The Spanish Fury, I thought. May the Lord deliver us from it.

We all sat silent in the longboat as we rowed back to the waiting *Aurora*. I huddled next to my hulking uncle and let the full extent of what we were doing flood over me. This could be it. This could be the final showdown with the *Red Queen*.

And Jack Steele.

I had actually seen the great pirate king before. Jessie and I had looked on when Steele killed a man as calmly as a normal man would kill a chicken. It was in Tortuga, when he had been masquerading as

Mr. Meade, the business manager for the man we saw him kill. I saw him again now in my mind's eye: tall, thin, pale as parchment, and wearing a long white wig. I'd often wondered if his real hair was as white, because for the life of me I couldn't imagine it being any other color. Still, what I remembered most were his eyes. They were a cold blue, like chips of winter ice, empty windows that opened to bleak death and destruction. Even in the smothering tropic heat I couldn't quite suppress a shudder.

Uncle Patch must have taken it for some fear of the coming battle, for he patted me awkwardly on the shoulder. "Don't let worry be a trouble to you, Davy," he whispered so the others wouldn't hear. "It's not fear, it's just good sense. In old Shakespeare's play about Henry IV, fat Falstaff said the better part of valor was discretion, you know. Sure, the brave know when to run and when to stand."

My uncle was completely wrong about what made me shudder, but he was a good man and he did try to understand. It was more than most would have done. So we sat until the great solid walls of the good old *Aurora* loomed up over us.

☠   ☠   ☠

That night I stood once again at the *Aurora*'s railing, watching the longboats setting out again on their missions. In the distance, the *Concepcion* did her best to blot out moon and stars, but I could just make out sleek shapes slipping away from her. They would be filled with Don Esteban's coldly efficient marines, and I almost fancied I saw the moonlight gleam off Sergeant Gonzalez's smile—all teeth, no humor.

I wish I could make a better show of myself, but I must admit that I was sulking. I would have sailed with our men even though I knew in my heart that for this kind of bloody work a boy was the last thing needed. And boy I was for all my work with Uncle Patch and my spying and problem solving. My thirteenth birthday was not quite two weeks away. Still, not being able to sail with the men gnawed at me and made me feel childish.

"You're sharp to go, are ye not?" asked my uncle, who could move silent as fog when he wished.

It was no use to deny it. "Aye."

He came to stand beside me in the darkness. "Would it do any good to say that dead doctors sew up no wounds?"

"It would not."

He gave his peculiar creaking chuckle. "One thing I will say for ye, Davy: Of all the Sheas, you must might be the most truthful."

I turned and looked at him, this man who was my only living relative. Captain Hunter had ordered that no lanterns were to be lit, but I could make Uncle Patch out in the darkness. He leaned there, slumped over the railing like a rumpled Irish bear.

"I saw you fight Shark," I said suddenly. "I knew you could use a sword, for I used to watch you spar with Captain Hunter. But I didn't know you were as good as that."

"Not good enough to keep from being clipped from behind as if I'd just fallen off a cart from County Clare."

"Where did you learn to fight, Uncle?"

For a short time he did not answer. Then, carelessly, he said, "'Tis a skill that lingers from my misspent youth at Trinity College in Dublin."

"And do they teach swordsmanship in college?"

"You'd be amazed what you can learn in college, my lad." Uncle Patch sniffed the night air and absently added, "And not all of it in a lecture hall.

Ah, we were a contentious lot in those days, and me more than most. I went out for duels at least once a month. 'Tis a wonder I've still got all my parts." He paused and stared into the silent night. "Did I ever tell you that I tried to call out Gerald? That I challenged him to a duel, though nothing came of it?"

"G-Gerald?" I stammered. "My father?"

"Your father, my brother, Gerald Shea, stalwart as an oak, thick as a brick. Oh, our quarrel was a high old Irish donnybrook, so it was, with us cursing each other, and your sainted mother, pretty Kathleen Sullivan she was then, in the middle of it whaling away at the two of us with a broomstick. She was a spirited girl, Kathleen Sullivan."

He fell silent again, and I asked, "But why did you quarrel at all?"

Uncle Patch grunted. "Oh, a vast host of reasons. I was a young wastrel squandering my talents and schooling. He was a fool and a prig for taking a commission in the army of the King of England. Mother favored him. Father favored me. The dog couldn't decide between the two of us. But most of all ..." Here his voice faded off for a moment. When he spoke again, it was no louder than a whisper.

"But most of all because sweet Kathleen Sullivan favored him over me. In the end, I stormed out of Ireland and into the navy, and never the two of them I saw again. The more fool I."

I stood there next to him, thankful that the night hid my face. Faith, my uncle had told me more about himself and my parents in five minutes than he had in a year. I swallowed and went for more. "He was always away from home, my father. Tell me, what was he like?"

"Take a look in a mirror, David Michael Shea, and sure he'll be looking back at you. I know he looks at me, only he does it through your sweet mother's hazel eyes, her gift to you. Ah, bless ye, Kathleen, ye made the right choice, though it tears my heart for me to confess it."

Then the still, hot night exploded, erupted into a column of fire that lit the sky up from sea to heaven. Moments later the sound slammed into us, seeming to squeeze the air from my lungs. Half deaf we stood there, my uncle pounding the railing with his fist.

"They've done it, by heaven and all the saints! They've done it! That was the powder magazine at Bloodhaven!"

CHAPTER 13

The Trap

BEFORE THE ECHOES of the great explosion had died away, Captain Hunter ordered the sails hoisted. Not half an hour passed before our three craft drew in close to land, and we could look in toward the harbor of Bloodhaven.

Fires raged there, rolling red and orange high into the night, and against the glare I could see the humped forms of the two fortified islands guarding the fairway. The nearer was long and smooth, and I thought of it as Hog Island, for it had the same shape as a sow half sunk in the mud. The farther one was harder to see, but it was smaller and rounder. Turtle Island, I decided, since it was like the back of a sea turtle.

Gazing between them into the harbor, I could see the black shapes of the anchored ships stark against the flames. And across the dark water came the crackle of gunfire. Captain Hunter tacked, making for the fairway, and I glanced nervously at Hog and Turtle Islands. "I hope Don Esteban's men have taken the forts."

At my shoulder my uncle said softly, "If they have not, we shall soon find out in the most unpleasant way."

Onward we glided, and suddenly the fortification atop Hog Island thundered with cannon fire. But it was not aimed at us. The guns had been hauled around to point toward the harbor, and they began to pound the shipping, the sloops and brigs that were fighting to win their anchors and put to sea.

And then the guns on Turtle Island, farther away, blazed out, but they clearly were striking at our friends on Hog Island. Don Esteban's marines had not taken that fort, after all.

"Silence those guns!" roared Captain Hunter. To starboard, the *Concepcíon* heeled suddenly, and at once I understood that Don Esteban had the same idea. She was closer, and her guns spoke before ours had a chance. The Turtle Island guns were now divided, some of them aiming at Hog Island, others at the *Concepcion,* and a few at the *Aurora* as we hauled up rapidly. I could smell the sharp reek of a sizzling slow match as the gunners bent over their weapons.

Then two guns on the island went off, revealing themselves in flashes of light, and our broadside rolled from bow to stern. It was too dark to see the flight and fall of cannonballs, but all of a sudden a red explosion blossomed on the face of the night like a burning rose, and our men sent up a hearty cheer. Our fire had found something, a store of powder, perhaps, and had set it alight.

"Torches!" bawled the lookout from the mast-head. "I see torches waving! Belay! Cease firing! I think our men have the island!"

Clearly they had part of it, for half the line of cannons on Turtle Island spoke no more. The *Concepcion* delivered one last broadside at the guns firing at her, and again an explosion lit the night. Against the light, I could see at least two tumbling cannon barrels. Within moments a bonfire flamed up on the island, and in its ruddy glare a gold-and-crimson flag ran up an improvised flagpole. It was Spanish. Don Esteban's men held both islands now, and a few longboats sped across the harbor, taking the last of the fleeing pirate defenders from Turtle Island.

From the quarterdeck I heard Captain Hunter growl, "If only the *Red Queen* were here!"

A brig and two sloops were making for us from the harbor, but as the Hog Island cannons opened on them, the brig quickly struck her colors. Shot crashed into both sloops, taking the mast from one and sending up fountains of water alongside the second. Both of the smaller craft tried to double back, with the dismasted one being rowed by its desperate crew. In the flickering light from the burning town I could see the deck of the brig, crowded with men holding their arms in the air.

I don't know how much time had passed since that first explosion. It seemed like nothing in one way, and in another it seemed as though the firing had been going on for hours and hours. But as we stood in toward the burning town, making slow work of it against a foul wind, I became aware that the sky was turning gray, the sun coming up astern of the ship. The wind from shore brought us the unpleasant odors of burning wood and powder, but I had the impression that the pirates in the town must have fled, for I heard no more gunfire.

And then the *Fury,* which had held back from the cannon fire, ranged alongside, with John Barrel clinging to the shrouds. "Ahoy!" he bawled in a voice that carried across the water. "Astern! Look astern! The *Red Queen* is bearing in!"

I sprang into the shrouds and climbed halfway to the mizzentop, gazing back over the water. Standing out against the growing light of dawn, an enormous black bulk of ship towered up from the sea. I felt the shrouds twitch, and my uncle laboriously clambered up to me, where he clung awkwardly, panting. "I must see this prodigy," he grunted.

"There," I said, pointing.

For a moment Uncle Patch was silent, holding his breath. Then he exhaled and whispered, "Sweet mother of—'tis clean impossible! Nothing that big can float!"

I knew how he felt. The skin of my arms crawled

as I realized the *Red Queen* was still a good two miles away. She loomed as though she were much closer. The *Concepcion,* to starboard of our ship, was so large that the *Aurora* looked like a fisherman's sloop next to her. But the *Red Queen* dwarfed even the *Concepcion.* She was so large that the *Aurora* could have been placed on her main deck with room to spare fore, aft, and to both sides.

Steele's ship was under a pyramid of billowed sails, standing in for all she was worth. I heard Captain Hunter bellowing orders, and our ship wore, turning away from the wind, to head toward this new threat. Don Esteban followed suit, but more slowly, for his ship could not maneuver so well as ours. I noticed that the *Fury,* the smallest of us all, was making for the security of Hog Island.

Uncle Patch and I scrambled back down to the deck, ran forward, and stood staring at the monster approaching us. The rim of the sun gleamed above the eastern horizon, first lighting her topgallants, then her topsails, and so down to the courses and decks. When the sun's rays struck her sides, the *Red Queen* became a crimson blaze, nearly glowing. Mr. Jeffers, the master gunner, came and whistled. "Three gun decks," he said softly. "And I make no doubt the bigger cannons throw thirty-two-, thirty-six-pound balls. Mates, she's a floating fortress, she is."

"God help us all," muttered my uncle. "That is what William proposes to fight!"

Despite all her sails the *Red Queen* made poor headway against the foul wind, for she stood only a matter of eight points free. That is, she could not sail directly toward us, for that would put the wind dead against her. Instead, the bloodred ship tacked, now swinging her prow to one side of the head-wind, now to the other.

The *Concepcíon,* after our turn, lay to the left, or larboard, of the *Aurora,* and one hundred yards away and astern of us. Uncle Patch and I hurried back to the quarterdeck. "William!" my uncle barked. "For the love of mercy, let Don Esteban catch up. If Steele hits us one at a time, we have not even a prayer."

Captain Hunter clenched his hands, staring ahead at the oncoming pirate ship. Then he nodded. "Very well." Raising his voice, he ordered, "Take a reef in the mainsail! Lower the topsails!"

It took only a few moments for the *Concepcíon* to

come abreast of us. Then the captain drew his sword. "Steady, lads! Steele means to sail right between us!"

I kept expecting my uncle to order me to accompany him below to the sick berth, which was our battle station. But he seemed frozen by the sight of the *Red Queen* and stood at the rail staring at her. I did not speak to him at all, but gazed at the figurehead of the closing ship, a woman dressed in flowing robes and wearing a crown. She had a billow of brilliant red hair, but where her face should have been I could see merely a grinning skull.

"Port your helm!" roared Captain Hunter. "Fire as they bear!"

The *Aurora* turned smoothly to the right, and beginning at the bows the guns went off one right after the other, a rippling crash. Jets of water leaped at the *Red Queen*'s waterline, and scarlet splinters flew from her bloodred hull where our guns struck true. At the same time, the *Concepción* had wheeled to larboard, and her own three decks of twenty-four-pound cannons blazed away. Some of her shot flew shockingly wild, but much of it battered into the *Red Queen*. Still the pirate ship came on, clearly meaning to sail between us and fire both sides.

We would be within pistol shot of her decks. We had fired two broadsides at her and were nearly ready with a third when her guns came within play. My uncle grabbed me by the scruff of my neck and thrust me down to the deck, falling beside me, as the *Red Queen* began to fire. The explosion of sound was incredible. I heard huge shot howling just overhead, or so it seemed, and heard the crash and crack of cannonballs hitting us.

But our cannons replied, at point-blank range. They stabbed into the open gunports of the pirate ship's lowest deck. Through the din I heard the clang of one of our cannonballs striking a gun or an anchor on the other ship. Men in our tops, armed with muskets, blazed away, though to hit anything on the *Red Queen*'s towering main deck they had to fire horizontally.

The *Red Queen* began to wear, turning her red bulk away from the wind and from us, and I guessed that Steele counted the larger *Concepcíon* as his main foe. The *Red Queen* lurched suddenly, for no reason that I could see until I realized that she had just fired her whole broadside at Don Esteban's ship. A moment later, the guns on our side fired again, but the shot mostly went wild, for the huge ship had heeled far over from the broadside opposite us.

Then we were past her stern, and I could see the *Concepcion* had taken great punishment. Her sails were rags, with broken spars dangling from every mast. Two of her gunports had been smashed into one. She was desperately turning to get her larboard broadside into action.

Captain Hunter's orders had brought us into a turn as well. Now both the *Aurora* and the *Concepcion* were astern of the *Red Queen*. The huge ship could not turn as nimbly as ours. Don Esteban and Captain Hunter were going to have a clear shot at the *Red Queen*'s starboard side.

We hammered her again, throwing everything we had, but to my eyes the striking cannonballs made no impression on the huge crimson ship. Don Esteban had given the order just that much too slowly, and before his gunners could fire, the *Red Queen* hit the *Concepcion* again, splinters flying and the fore-topmast plunging down. But the Spanish gunners loosed a broadside, smashing hard into the *Red Queen*'s bows.

The top row of Steele's guns went off then, aiming over the *Concepcion* and at us. The shot whistled high, but struck the mizzenmast at the partners. The sharpshooters in the top screamed as the mast toppled, and a tangle of splintered spars and cordage thumped to the quarterdeck, barely missing Captain Hunter.

The *Red Queen* fled ahead of us now, standing off and making good time to the east. Clearly Steele knew his position and realized he could not fight two fortified islands and three vessels at once. I ran forward, ducking dangling lines and leaping over an upset cannon, until I reached the bowsprit and clambered out onto it. I could see a figure aboard the *Red Queen* looking backward at us over the gold-and-scarlet taffrail. It was a thin man with long silvery white hair or a wig. He caught sight of me and mockingly drew a rapier and lifted it in a duelist's salute. But I could see no humor in the somber face of Jack Steele.

I hurried back to my uncle. Captain Hunter had climbed into the rigging, but now he dropped back to the deck. "He got away!" he shouted in a voice of despair. His words came faintly to me, for my ears were numb from the thunderous din of battle.

Uncle Patch clapped a hand onto his shoulder. In a hoarse shout, he said, "Aye, but you've hurt him badly, William! You've hit him hard twice. You've deprived him of two safe havens, and sure, that's more than all the navies in the world have done. Come away, now, come away! Your ship needs ye."

Captain Hunter pounded the rail with his fist. "I shall find him again, I swear it. I will never rest until the bloody *Red Queen* lies on the bottom of the sea, with Jack Steele in her arms!"

Across an expanse of sea, the *Concepcíon* was desperately signaling her need of carpenters. She listed to starboard, obviously taking on water. The *Fury* came closing in to help, and I saw Chips, our carpenter, loading a skiff as he and his crew prepared to row across.

Then my uncle said, "Come, Davy. We've wounded to tend, and that's a man's business too."

As we worked over the wounds of our shipmates, I could not help saying, "We failed, Uncle. We failed to take him."

Uncle Patch did not look up from the gash he was stitching. Through the wind port sunlight streamed, gleaming in his coppery red hair. Patiently he said, "There is nothing like complete success this side of heaven, lad, and nothing like complete failure this side of perdition. We have dealt the pirate king Steele a blow from which he will never recover."

"But he's free!"

"Aye," said my uncle, neatly tying off his last stitch. "A tot of rum for Mr. Grady, Davy, that's a good lad. Who's next?"

A gunner with a scorched hand took Mr. Grady's place, and as he prepared a salve, my uncle said, as if no interruption had occurred, "Aye, Steele sails out there, and free, but here we are, our joints sound and whole. And now Steele sails all alone, Davy. We've taken his navy from him, and his harbors are closed or destroyed. 'Tis a terrible fate for any man to be all alone. It will be worse for Steele, for not even a pirate will trust him now."

When we finished our work, we came back onto the deck. It was noon by that time. The wreckage had been cleared overboard, and we were about to anchor in the lee of Hog Island, so that our own repairs could begin. Men thronged the yardarms and deck, lowering sails, preparing to drop the anchors.

But on the quarterdeck, his hands behind his back, his head bowed, stood Captain Hunter.

And looking at him, I could not help but think, This man, too, sails alone.

The Red Queen

Jack Steele's fearsome pirate ship is of a type that did not really exist until a little later in naval history. In the late 1600s, ships were beginning to change, becoming faster, sleeker, and more maneuverable. It is surprising to many people that the ship's wheel, the spoked steering wheel, was not invented until the early 1700s. Until that time smaller vessels were steered by tillers. These were levers attached to the rudder. Moving the lever to the right caused the rudder to turn to the left, which steered the ship to the left. Larger ships used a vertical lever called a whipstaff. The invention of the ship's wheel would lead to ships that were easier to turn and more effective in battle.

Something like that improvement is at work with the *Red Queen*. She was a Spanish galleon, and so was among the largest ships sailing the American seas during the 1600s. However, the Spanish were very conservative in building their ships. Galleons had a high forecastle in the front and a very high aftercastle in the back. In a way, that gave them an advantage in combat, because the high-mounted guns in the aftercastle could fire down at an enemy ship. However, the tall structure caught the wind and made the ship hard to maneuver and slow to turn.

Jack Steele cut off the higher decks from both the front and the rear of the *Red Queen*. She still had three rows of huge guns. After Steele redesigned the ship, she could turn almost as fast as a frigate, which was a much smaller vessel with only one deck that carried guns. And the loss of the high aftercastle meant that she could spread more sails and sail along at a very rapid rate. Steele took a ship that was meant to carry and protect treasure and turned it into a ship of prey. With its speed, heavy cannons, huge crew, and maneuverability, the *Red Queen* would have been a terror of the seas, and years ahead of her time.

Part of our inspiration for this improvement in ship building came from many years after the *Red*

Queen's era. The USS *Constitution*, built for the United States Navy in 1797, was similarly ahead of her time. With her unusually thick hull, she could withstand enemy fire. The cannonballs often bounced off, giving her the nickname "Old Ironsides." Her cannons were large and well-aimed. She carried a fierce array of them. Her standard armament called for forty-four heavy cannons, but she has carried as many as fifty-two, far beyond the British standard of twenty-eight or thirty-two guns on their frigates. She was also bigger than British frigates. As the saying went, she was big enough to defeat anything smaller, and fast enough to outrun anything larger. Like the *Red Queen*, "Old Ironsides" was never defeated in her many battles. She was so well built that she is still afloat today in Boston Harbor. In fact, after more than two hundred years she is still a ship on active duty in the United States Navy!

—Brad Strickland and Thomas E. Fuller,
September 2002

Biographies

BRAD STRICKLAND has written or cowritten nearly fifty novels. He and Thomas E. Fuller have worked together on many books about Wishbone, TV's literature-loving dog, and Brad and his wife Barbara have also written books featuring Sabrina, the Teenage Witch, the mystery-solving Shelby Woo, and characters from *Star Trek*. On his own, Brad has written mysteries, science fiction, and fantasy novels. When he is not writing, Brad is a Professor of English at Gainesville College in Oakwood, Georgia. He and Barbara have a daughter, Amy, a son, Jonathan, and a daughter-in-law, Rebecca. They also have a house full of pets, including two dogs, three cats, a ferret, a gerbil, and two goldfish, one named George W. Bush and one named Fluffy.

THOMAS E. FULLER has been co-authoring young adult novels with Brad Strickland for the last five years. They are best known for their work on the Wishbone mysteries as well as a number of radio dramas and published short stories. Otherwise, Thomas is best known as the head writer of the Atlanta Radio Theatre Company. He has won awards for his adaptation of H. G. Wells's "The Island of Dr. Moreau," his original drama, "The Brides of Dracula," and the occult Western, "All Hallow's Moon." Thomas lives in Duluth, Georgia, in a slightly shabby blue house full of books, manuscripts, audio tapes, and too many children, including his sons Edward, Anthony, and John, and occasionally his daughter, Christina.

PENDRAGON

Bobby Pendragon is a seemingly normal fourteen-year-old boy. He has a family, a home, and a possible new girlfriend. But something happens to Bobby that changes his life forever.

HE IS CHOSEN TO DETERMINE THE COURSE OF HUMAN EXISTENCE.

Pulled away from the comfort of his family and suburban home, Bobby is launched into the middle of an immense, inter-dimensional conflict involving racial tensions, threatened ecosystems, and more. It's a journey of danger and discovery for Bobby, and his success or failure will do nothing less than determine the fate of the world. . . .

PENDRAGON

From Aladdin Paperbacks
Published by Simon & Schuster